BEWARE!:
DO NOT READ THIS
BOOK FROM
BEGINNING TO END!

Bummer! You have to take your bratty little sister Joanie with you to the mall. Before you and your friend Sid can stop her, Joanie runs into a magic shop. Of course, she touches everything in the store. But when Joanie leaves the shop carrying a big book of magic spells, you know you're headed for trouble. Big trouble!

The book of spells belongs to an evil magician. And he's going to use every terrifying magic trick — sawing you in half, throwing knives at you, even setting hundreds of rabbits loose — to get his book back! Time is running out. The magician has put a powerful spell on Joanie — her body is slowly evaporating. And you're next!

Can you destroy the magician before he waves his wand and makes you disappear into thin air?

You're in control of this scary adventure. You decide what will happen. And how terrifying the scares will be!

Start on page 1. Then follow the instructions at the bottom of each page. You make the choices.

SO TAKE A DEEP BREATH. CROSS YOUR FINGERS. AND TURN TO PAGE 1 NOW TO *GIVE YOURSELF GOOSEBUMPS!*

**READER BEWARE —
YOU CHOOSE THE SCARE!**

Look for more
GIVE YOURSELF GOOSEBUMPS adventures
from R.L. STINE:

R.L. STINE
GIVE YOURSELF

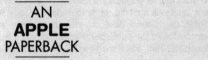

UNDER THE MAGICIAN'S SPELL

AN
APPLE
PAPERBACK

SCHOLASTIC INC.
New York Toronto London Auckland Sydney

ISBN 0-590-67321-1

12 11 10 9 8 7 6 5 4 3 2 1   6 7 8 9/9 0 1/0

Printed in the U.S.A.   40

First Scholastic printing, July 1996

You flatten yourself against the wall. You listen hard for a noise — any noise. Will you be able to make your escape?

The only sound you hear is your own raspy breathing. You slowly peer around the corner. All clear. "It's now or never," you murmur.

You take a deep breath and sprint toward freedom.

Bang! The door slams behind you as you fling yourself onto the lawn.

"Made it!" you cheer. But you know there's no time to celebrate. You glance around. So far so good. You race around the side of the house.

And come to a dead stop.

Turn to PAGE 2.

There they are. Standing right by your bicycle.
Your mother and your little sister, Joanie.

"Hi, sweetie," your mother greets you. "Where
are you off to in such a hurry?"

Your stomach sinks to your toes. You were so
close. So close to escape. Now you know what's
coming.

"I'm meeting Sid at the mall," you mumble to
your mom.

"That sounds like fun, dear. I'm sure Joanie
would like to go, too."

"Maaaa!" you wail. "Joanie is such a pain! She
gets into everything. I have to watch her every
second!"

"Joanie will behave, won't you, cutie?" Your
mother turns to Joanie and kisses her cheek.

Joanie nods sweetly. She gives you a big fake
smile.

Good-bye fun, you think.

Your bratty nine-year-old sister always gets
you into trouble. She has to touch everything she
sees. "Break it or take it" seems to be Joanie's
motto. But she's so disgustingly cute, no one ever
seems to get mad at her. Grown-ups love her
brown curls and bright blue eyes.

"Look, Joanie wants to hold your hand," your
mother gushes. "Isn't that cute?"

Before you puke, turn to PAGE 3.

You shake off Joanie's hand. Once your mother is out of sight, you know Joanie will drop her cutie-pie routine.

"Listen up, Joanie," you tell her. "I'm in charge. So hurry up and grab your bike. I'm already late."

"I have to get my diary first," Joanie says.

That stupid diary. Joanie never goes anywhere without it.

"You two have fun," your mother tells you. Then she follows Joanie into the house.

"Joanie," you holler. "I'm leaving. NOW!" You jump on your bike and pedal as fast as you can. Hopefully none of your friends will spot you riding to the mall with your little sister. You glance back and see that Joanie is pedaling hard to keep up with you.

When you reach the mall, you and Joanie lock your bikes in the rack. "Don't wander off," you instruct Joanie.

"Who, me?" she asks super-sweetly.

Hurry to PAGE 18.

How can a guy without a head choke you? But the fingers at your throat tighten their grip!

"Help me," you manage to choke out.

Joanie finds a sword on the wall and chops off the Magician's arm. You and the arm fall to the ground. Then Joanie pries the Magician's fingers off your neck.

"Thanks," you tell Joanie. "That was close."

You stand up and walk over to the head. "Yuck," you say, picking it up. You bring it over to the cabinet and place it on the empty shelf.

It's over.

"What's going on?" Sid asks. He is sitting on the guillotine. The trance must have been broken when you defeated the Magician.

"It's a long story," you say.

Then you notice something. The walls of the shop seem to be dissolving around you. You, Joanie, and Sid hurry out the door. You turn back and see that the Magic Shop has already disappeared. You glance down at the Magic Book in your hand — it's fading away to nothing!

Well, after a day like today, maybe you're not so surprised after all.

THE END

"Where's my sister?" you demand, racing into the room.

The giant smiles his creepy smile at you. "You're just in time for the show," he says.

That's when you notice the kid next to Sid isn't a real kid. It's a ventriloquist's dummy. A really ugly dummy.

"Where's Joanie?" you ask again. Of course, knowing Joanie, she could have wandered off by herself.

The dummy's red eyes blink open. "I'm Freaky Freddie," the dummy says. "Children don't like me. They think I'm too scary to look at."

"Sid, come on," you say. "We have to find Joanie."

But Sid just stares blankly ahead. It's as if he were made out of wood.

Uh-oh.

"I need cuter dummies for my act," the giant explains. "Then people will like me."

No, you think. It can't be! You notice a large cabinet. You rush toward it and yank it open.

"Joanie!" you shriek. She gazes at you silently. She's a dummy! And crumpled beside her is another dummy. You pick it up and gasp in horror!

The dummy has *your* face!

You now know how this will

END.

"Joanie," you spit out through clenched teeth. "We've only just arrived, and already you've — "

You're interrupted by a poke in the back. You whirl around. There's Sid with a goofy smile on his face.

"Ooooops," Sid says sheepishly. He holds up his hands. They're handcuffed together.

"Sid," you scold him. "You're as bad as Joanie!"

A booming voice makes you jump. "I see that you are enjoying my magic tricks."

Great, you think. The store owner. Now we'll have to pay for the tricks we've touched. But where is the guy? You glance around the shop. You don't see anyone. You smell something though. Something musty and rotten.

"Welcome to the Magic Shop," the voice says. A tall, thin man with a skinny mustache steps out of the shadows. He's dressed all in black. His black cape swirls around him as if there were a strong wind blowing.

Except, you remind yourself, we're indoors.

"I am the Magician," the tall man declares.

Turn to PAGE 125.

Joanie has already disappeared. Too bad you can't just let her stay lost. You glance around the mall.

"There she is," you say, pointing across the courtyard.

Joanie stands frozen in front of a shop window as if she were in a trance. For a moment you could swear her feet are floating inches off the floor.

Can't be, you tell yourself. You blink and look again. No, her feet are still on the ground.

"The Magic Shop." You read the store's sign aloud.

"She's going in," Sid warns.

"Come on," you cry. "We've got to get her out of there. That store won't know what hit it."

You and Sid follow Joanie into the Magic Shop. It takes a few seconds for your eyes to adjust to the dim light.

Sid gives a little gasp beside you. "Wow," you murmur. The shop is filled from floor to ceiling with magic tricks.

Of course, Joanie is touching every single one.

You shake your head as you watch her fiddling with a miniature guillotine. But then she sticks her finger into place under the tiny blade.

"Joanie, don't!" you shout.

Before you can stop her, she pulls the string. The blade drops right through her finger!

Rush over to PAGE 114!

"Hey!" you exclaim. "Where did he go?"

Sid points toward a black curtain at the rear of the shop. You walk up to the curtain and give it a yank. There's nothing behind it but a solid brick wall!

Weird.

"It's time to leave," you tell Sid. He agrees. You quickly find Joanie kneeling in front of a huge bookcase.

"Come on, Joanie, we're going," you tell her.

"But I'm — "

"Now!" you command, yanking her to her feet.

"We need to remove Sid's handcuffs," you say once you're outside. "We have some tools back at our clubhouse."

"Maybe this will help," Joanie says. She holds up an old book. The words *Magic Book of Spells* are written across the gold cover.

"Joanie!" you screech. "What are you doing with that?"

"I tried to tell you," Joanie whines. "But you dragged me out of the store. Besides, I think there's a spell in here for getting out of handcuffs."

"Well, somebody needs to do something," Sid grumbles. "I think these cuffs are getting tighter." What should you do?

If you decide to try a spell from the book, turn to PAGE 32.

If you decide to go back to the clubhouse and use regular tools, turn to PAGE 47.

"Let's get out of here!" you tell Joanie and Sid. You grab their arms and pull them away from Larry's front door.

The three of you hide behind a tall row of hedges.

"So what are we going to do now?" Sid demands.

"I don't know. I'm thinking," you reply.

"You're the one who got us into this mess," Sid declares.

"Me?" you cry.

"Yeah, you. If you hadn't brought your little sister to the mall with us, then . . . "

You and Sid argue and argue.

Suddenly you realize that Joanie has been quiet for a long time. Too long.

You turn to stare at your sister.

Oh, no! Time has run out!

While you and Sid were arguing, Joanie has been disappearing and disappearing and disappearing.

And now you can't see her at all.

THE END

The red ball! It's not there!

"You lose," Mr. Knowledge announces.

"Not so fast," Joanie demands. "The game is not over yet. You have to show us what's under the other cups."

"Do not!" Mr. Knowledge sneers.

"Do too!" Joanie insists. "Or else you'll be known as a cheater!"

You grab the middle cup and lift it up. No red ball. Sid picks up the left cup. Nothing. You've been tricked!

"Cheater!" Sid yells. You and Joanie join in, chanting, "Cheater! Cheater!" You point accusing fingers at Mr. Knowledge.

"*Grrrrr! Mmmurrkkk!*" Awful sounds burst from Mr. Knowledge's mouth. His hair turns gray and stringy. He grows at least two feet. His face swells up into a puffy mask with yellow slime running out of his eyes and nose.

He reaches out with one enormous monster hand and grabs Joanie.

"Appetizer!" he grunts. Before Joanie can scream, he pops her into his mouth.

"Main course!" the monster booms, grabbing Sid. He eats Sid in one bite.

"Dessert," the monster says, reaching for you. You guessed it. This is

THE END.

The horrible laughter fills your ears. The rotting smell fills your nose. And then there he is in front of you.

The Magician.

"There's no escape," he sneers. He grabs the hourglass around your neck and pulls hard. The cord snaps.

"Just a few more grains of sand left," he says, holding up the hourglass for you to see. "Then I'll have three new heads for my collection."

The Magician waves his hand. The wooden cabinet appears. He snaps his fingers. The doors fly open. The terrible shrunken heads stare out at you.

"The chubby one will go first," the Magician says. You hear a clanking of metal wheels. You gasp! A real guillotine rolls into the center of the room!

Go to PAGE 80.

There's no way you're climbing into that Dumpster! You're going into the factory. You, Joanie, and Sid creep up to the door. You jiggle the handle. It's locked.

"Now what?" you ask.

"The fire escape," Sid says. You glance up at the fire escape. Most of the guardrails have broken away and several of the metal steps are missing. The nails that anchor the steps to the brick wall are rusty. There is a metal ladder attached to the bottom step. It's about three feet over your head.

"I'll go first," you say. "Give me a boost."

You place a hand on Joanie's shoulder to steady yourself. Sid locks his fingers together. You place your foot in his hands. He boosts you up. You grab the bottom rail and pull yourself the rest of the way.

You step onto the fire escape. It wobbles, swinging from side to side.

You find the release mechanism for the ladder, and it drops down. It makes a terrible groaning sound, but it still works. Sid and Joanie carefully climb up behind you. When you reach the second floor, you find a broken window.

You peer inside but it's too dark to see anything but shadowy shapes. You climb in through the window.

Two shiny yellow eyes greet you.

Turn to PAGE 118.

You feel light-headed. You are about to faint. There's something you should do. But you can't think. Oh, what is it?

More tentacles swirl around your body. You're being slowly drawn forward into the mass of worms.

Just as you are about to be devoured by the mass of tiny worm mouths, you remember what it was you were supposed to do.

You forgot to scream. You forgot to give the warning to Sid and Joanie. That means they'll take this path, thinking it is the Safe Path.

It had been such a good plan. If only it had worked. . . .

THE END

You don't think you'll be able to steal back the Magic Book. Larry must have hidden it somewhere by now. Your only choice is to buy it from him. But you have a problem.

"How are we going to raise $50?" Sid asks.

That's a tough one.

You look over at Joanie, thinking hard. If you don't get the book back, Joanie will disappear in an hour.

You shiver with fear. But you can't let the fear clog your brain. You've gotten out of tougher situations before.

"I know," Joanie pipes up. "You can sell some of your CDs. You've got a million of them. And all the music you listen to stinks."

You stare at Joanie as if she were crazy.

"I've got a better idea," you tell her. "Why don't you sell your collection of Barbie doll designer clothes? Why does she need five coats? Are you afraid she'll get cold?"

"Shut up!"

"No, *you* shut up!"

Luckily, Sid interrupts you. "I've got an idea!" he shouts over your argument.

Turn to PAGE 37.

So you think the ball is under the middle cup.
WRONG!

But you can have another chance to guess again.

And this time, pay attention! Keep your eye on that little red ball.

Turn to PAGE 26.

You decide to let the scorpion finish off the Magician.

You hear the scorpion slither forward.

Go to it, you think. Eat the Magician. Crunch him to bits. Swallow him whole. Sting him with your poison stinger.

The scorpion slides past you, right up to the Magician.

You're going to enjoy this.

"Hey, pal," the scorpion greets the Magician.

Any minute now, you think.

"Ah, my old friend," the Magician answers. "How are you?"

This isn't going the way you imagined it.

"So what are we going to do with this pesky kid?" the scorpion asks the Magician.

"Wait!" you cry out. "I thought you were going to save me. This is the Scorpion Safetyway!"

"Sorry," the scorpion tells you. "But I'm off-duty."

THE END

"Look out!" you shout. The balls of fire speed toward you. You put your hands in front of your face. You catch a fireball and toss it back. Before you can take a breath, the jugglers throw another fireball at you. Once again, you manage to toss it back.

Why aren't my hands burning up? you wonder. You notice Sid and Joanie gazing at you in awe.

The jugglers surround you. Somehow you manage to return every ball they throw. As you toss the flaming balls in the air, the jugglers speak in eerie flat tones.

"We," says one juggler.

"Know," says the second.

"Who you are," says the third.

"What do you mean — *yeowch!*" It's hard to talk and juggle at the same time. You drop the fiery ball and — *poof!* — all the other balls vanish.

"You took the Magician's book," the first juggler says.

"The Magician wants it back," says the second.

"Then he'll eat you for dinner," says the third.

Turn to PAGE 64.

18

You roll your eyes at Joanie's sickly-sweet act. You rush through the mall to meet your friend Sid. You spot him pacing in front of The Comic Connection. Sid is wearing a blue jacket that is a little too small for his chubby frame. He runs a hand through his spiky blond hair. "Where were you?" he demands as you hurry over to him.

"My mom made me bring Joanie," you explain.

"Really?" Sid raises an eyebrow. "Then where is the little princess?"

Oh, no! Did you lose Joanie already?

Turn to PAGE 7.

"Sid. Joanie," you whisper. "If none of us said that, and the bird didn't say that, who said that?"

"The Magician?" Joanie squeaks.

The three of you turn slowly and scan the room.

A man steps out of the shadows. It's not the Magician. But you don't feel any better. This is the biggest, grossest-looking guy you've ever seen.

His massive body towers over you. Your eyes travel up, up, up to the man's face. His skin is the color your face turns when you're about to be sick. Drool runs out of the corner of his mouth. You can smell his foul breath from across the room. He is one creepy dude. And he doesn't look happy.

We're in big trouble, you think.

The giant's voice booms: "GIVE ME MY BIRDIE!"

Turn to PAGE 65.

You decide it's easier to climb down the rope ladder.

You untangle yourself and start down. When you slide to the bottom, you motion to Sid and Joanie to follow you. Your feet hit the ground. You quickly duck behind some boxes.

You can hear Larry, D. J., and Buddy joking up ahead. Luckily, there are piles of cardboard boxes stacked around the warehouse, so the bullies haven't noticed you.

Yet.

You, Sid, and Joanie tiptoe behind the stacked boxes. You peer around the side.

D. J. and Buddy are sprawled a few feet ahead of you. They're laughing and punching each other in the arms. Larry has the Magic Book in his hands. His lips appear to be moving.

That's when you realize what is going on.

"Larry is reading one of the magic spells," you tell Sid and Joanie.

Turn to PAGE 42.

"What's wrong with me?" you ask. You try to stand up, but your muscles don't seem to be working.

You hear a gasp. Sid and Joanie rush toward you. The Masked Man holds out his hand and helps you to your feet.

You glance down. Your mouth drops open in horror.

Your feet! Your feet are on backwards!

You turn to the Masked Man. "What did you do to me?" you demand.

"The trick was going so well," he explains. "I sawed you in half without a problem. But then . . . " He shrugs his shoulders.

Sid and Joanie crowd around you. "You have to fix this!" Sid shouts. Joanie gazes at your backward bottom half in awe.

"I can try," the Masked Man says. He picks up the saw.

"No way!" you yell. "Who knows what kind of mistake he'll make next time!"

"Well," Joanie says, "Mom always complains that you don't know if you're coming or going. Now you have an excuse!"

THE END

"Maybe the fishbowl would be a good place to hide the Magic Book," you say. You walk over to the shelf and peer at the fishbowl. The fish stare back.

"No way," Joanie says. "It will be totally obvious."

"And the fish might get mad," Sid adds.

"I don't think that's going to happen," you tell them. You've just noticed the fish aren't real. They're just painted on the inside of the clear bowl. You reach into it.

And do a double-take. You can't believe what you see! Your hand becomes invisible inside the fishbowl! It disappears completely.

You test it again. You pull your hand out of the bowl, shake off the water, and then stick it back in. It disappears again. This is so cool!

"Hey, Joanie!" you shout. "Check this out."

Joanie glances your way. You watch her eyes travel down your arm to the fishbowl. Her mouth drops when she notices that your hand appears to be gone!

Then you lift your arm out of the water. Joanie's eyes grow wide with terror. You glance down at the end of your arm where your hand *should* be.

"My hand," you gasp. "Where's my hand?"

Turn to PAGE 106.

Granny's rough treatment is starting to annoy you.

"Let me help you there," Granny Kapusta says in her crackly voice. As she yanks you to your feet, you spot something on the floor. It looks like a tooth.

Granny Kapusta pushes you in front of her. That creepy feeling is back. You glance at Granny. She has stopped to pull shut a window curtain and doesn't notice you watching her.

You don't believe it! Her blue eyes — they turned yellow! It was just for a second, but you know what you saw. That's it, you think. We've got to get out of this house before it's too late.

But how?

Your eyes dart around the hallway searching for some escape route. There's an open door up ahead. It might be your only chance to get out of here alive.

Do you want to escape by going through the door? Go to PAGE 33.

If you want to go into the kitchen to grab the Pat the Rat, go to PAGE 89.

Too bad. This isn't your lucky day.

"Ha ha ha ha ha!"

Oh, no! It didn't work — the Magician is still alive!

But where is he?

You eye the crumpled cape. He couldn't still be under there, could he?

You creep toward the cape. It's just a piece of fabric, you tell yourself. You try to shake off a feeling of dread as you move slowly forward.

CLINK! Your foot accidentally hits the hourglass that was sitting on the floor. It skitters across the room, stopping in front of the cape.

You reach out for the hourglass. But another hand clutches it first. A hand that stretches out from under the cape.

The Magician's hand!

Turn to PAGE 51.

Come on, you know better than that! If you touch a hair on Joanie's head, you'll be grounded for life and you won't be able to finish the rest of the adventure. So take a deep breath, count to ten, and be nice to your little sister.

Go on. You can do it.

Go back to PAGE 6.

"What's a henway?" Mr. Knowledge repeats the question.

You can't help yourself. "A hen weighs about six pounds," you shout from the audience. You love these old jokes.

Mr. Knowledge gazes out at the audience. "Very good, my young friend. You may ask the next question."

You know exactly what to ask. "How do we escape from here?"

Mr. Knowledge looks startled. "That is an interesting question. It requires an interesting answer. Please, join me onstage."

You, Joanie, and Sid race up to the stage. When you are standing beside Mr. Knowledge you are amazed to see that the entire audience has vanished.

"The answer to your question is in the red ball," Mr. Knowledge explains. He pulls a small red ball from his pocket and places it on the table in front of him. From a drawer in the table, he produces three small cups. He puts them in a row — one cup on the right, one cup in the middle, and one cup on the left.

Then Mr. Knowledge takes the red ball and places it under the middle cup.

Now what?

Find out on PAGE 87.

The curse of the Magic Book must be working. Joanie is disappearing! You don't want to scare her, so you don't say anything about her missing ears.

But you'd better get that book back — fast!

"Okay, back to the plan," you say. "Let's track down those jerks and find out what they've done with the Magic Book."

"*Shh,*" Joanie hisses. "I hear something."

You and Sid lie down with your ears to the floor. No mistaking that laugh. Larry, D. J., and Buddy are downstairs.

You creep toward the center of the room where you think you'll be able to hear them better. The floor squeaks under your feet. You try picking your feet up, high, as if you were marching, and putting them down slowly.

It's working. No more squeaks. Foot up — foot down. Foot up — but this time there is no floor beneath your foot!

You desperately try to balance yourself on the edge of the hole in the floor. Your knees start to shake. Back and forth you sway. You try to steady yourself, using your arms for balance.

It doesn't work. You're falling into the open space, down toward the hard cement floor below you!

Turn to PAGE 127.

You can't juggle? That's okay. Not too many people can. It's really hard!

But this is a story about magic. So now, PRESTO! you can magically juggle!

Turn to PAGE 17.

You've got it! You grab the Magic Book from the floor of the Dumpster. But you lose your balance. Your arms and legs fly out in the air as you sink down into the trash.

You scrunch up your face to avoid breathing in the awful stench. You open one eye and prop yourself up on one elbow.

Two red eyes peer back at you.

A long, twitchy nose is inches away from your face.

You are staring at the biggest rat you've ever seen. This rat is the size of a sheepdog!

You fling yourself as hard as you can to the other side of the Dumpster. But it's no good. You slip and slide on the slimy trash. You don't even have time to let out a scream when the monster rat lunges for your throat.

THE END

It's a trick, you tell yourself. But how does it work?

A second sword pierces the cabinet. Without thinking, you lift your foot and step onto the sword as it slices through to the other side. Somehow, it manages to hold your weight.

That's it, you realize. I have to step on each sword as it comes through the cabinet wall.

It's difficult, but you manage to keep your balance as you climb on top of each sword that slides into the cabinet. By the time the final sword is pushed through, you are crouching in a tiny space at the top.

Now what? you wonder.

Then the swords are slowly pulled out again. As each sword slides out, you place a foot on the sword below it.

Finally, you are standing again at the bottom of the cabinet. The door flings open.

"Excellent!" The Masked Man congratulates you. "Such good work should be rewarded. What is it you want?"

"We want to get out of here," you tell the Masked Man. "How do we escape this crazy place?"

The Masked Man gazes at you sadly. "I'm sorry, but I can't tell you that."

Turn to PAGE 50.

Sid looks terrible. His face is the color of paste. His eyes are squeezed tightly shut. His mouth is wrinkled up in a tight grimace.

"What's wrong, Sid?" you ask. But you think you already know the answer.

"I don't like small spaces," he whispers.

That's what you were afraid of.

"Are you claustrophobic?" Joanie asks. "Do you have a terrible fear of close spaces? Do you feel like you can't breathe? That we're running out of air in here, and you're about to suffocate?"

Sid's hands reach out for Joanie's throat. You grab Sid's wrists. "Cut it out," you warn them.

This is just great, you think. Sid is about to go ballistic. You're trapped inside a cardboard box. What else could go wrong?

You're about to find out.

Turn to PAGE 122.

"Okay, let's see if we can find a spell that will do the trick," you say. You're willing to try anything. You grab the small, gold-covered book from Joanie and skim the pages.

"It must be written in some kind of code," you say. "I've never seen words like this before."

"I bet I can read it," Joanie brags, grabbing the book back from you. "Let me have it."

"Fine, smarty-pants," you say. "Go ahead."

Joanie studies the book, turning the pages slowly. "It must be a foreign language," she says finally.

"Yeah, like Transylvanian," Sid jokes. "Maybe the English translation is in the back of the book."

Joanie flips to the back pages. "I think you're right," she says. "This looks like English."

You peer at the book over her shoulder. "Oh right," you say sarcastically. You snatch the book back from her. "If this is English, then what does '*Ibin dos yaget nobis tagoo*' mean?"

Unfortunately, you are about to find out.

Go to PAGE 40.

That door looks like your only chance to escape.

There's no time to explain to Sid and Joanie what you're doing. You grab their hands and begin to run. You push them through the open door. Then you slam it behind you. You slide the bolt shut. Joanie and Sid stare at you as if you were crazy.

You put your finger to your lips, listening at the door. Horrible growling sounds start coming from the other side.

"Come out of there!" Granny bellows. Then claws scrape against the door.

"Granny doesn't sound so friendly anymore," Sid says nervously.

You feel around in the dark and find a light switch. A single lightbulb flashes on. You are at the top of cement steps leading into a cellar. You glance around the damp room. You're in luck! You notice a small window, high up near the ceiling. And it's open!

"We can get out that way," you tell Sid and Joanie, "but we need something to climb on."

"There, on the other side of the cellar," Sid points out. "Those dry pet food bags."

You and Sid cross to the stack of bags. Then you notice what's written on them. *Wild Wolf Chow.*

Turn to PAGE 72.

The Magician will be here any minute!

"Those jugglers made it sound like we're goners," Sid whispers to you.

"Even if we give him back his book," Joanie adds glumly.

You've got to act fast. But you can't escape because you don't know where you are. Besides, there doesn't seem to be a normal door in this black room. Your only hope is to hide the book. Then the Magician will need you alive if he wants the book back.

"We've got to hide the book," you tell Sid and Joanie. "I'm going to put it in the coffin."

"No," Sid says. "It will be too easy to find. Let's look around."

You search the room for a hiding place. There isn't much choice. A wide shelf runs along one wall. On it sits a large fishbowl with three exotic fish and an old-fashioned metal birdcage with a yellow canary.

If you still think the coffin is the best place to hide the book, go to PAGE 101.

If you hide the book in the fishbowl, turn to PAGE 22.

If you put the book in the birdcage, turn to PAGE 132.

You open your eyes and sneak another look at the cowboy. It's hard to see his face as you spin round and round. He seems to be concentrating very hard.

"Is this trick safe?" Joanie asks, her voice trembling. She sounds scared. It's kind of nice to know she's worried about you.

"I'll tell you a secret, young lady," the cowboy assures her. "It's a trick knife. Completely harmless."

"Cool," Sid says. He and Joanie lean forward in their seats.

Maybe the cowboy knows what he's doing, you think. You've seen this act in circuses before.

You shut your eyes just before the cowboy throws the knife.

"Ooooops! Wrong knife!" are the last words you ever hear.

THE END

You don't think the Magician will let you go once you give him the book. Your best bet is to escape now. But how?

"If the Magician got out," you say, "so can we!"

"But he's magic," Joanie counters. "And he knows his way around. He probably *built* this creepy room!"

"Fine," you tell her, "*don't* help. Your pointy little head will look great on that shelf."

Joanie stamps her feet. The hollow sound echoes in the small room. "Quit picking on me," she whines.

You and Sid roll your eyes. "Come on, Sid," you say. "Maybe we can find some sort of trapdoor." You begin tapping on the brick wall, searching for a hidden door.

Joanie stomps over to the corner. She sits there and pouts.

You ignore her and wave at the coffin. "This stuff had to be brought in here somehow," you tell Sid. You have a nagging feeling that you had the solution a minute ago, but it slipped away.

Joanie's singing TV jingles. She's *so* annoying.

"Joanie, cut it out!" you yell. "We're trying to — " Then something occurs to you. As strange as it seems, you think the answer is in something Joanie said or did.

Is the clue in something Joanie said? Find out on PAGE 46.

Is the clue in something Joanie did? Turn to PAGE 108.

"Let's steal something from Larry," Sid suggests. "Something that he would be willing to trade for the Magic Book."

"That's an awesome idea," you tell Sid.

"But what are we going to take from Larry?" asks Joanie. "And how are we going to get it without anyone knowing?"

"Don't worry," you reassure Joanie. "I know exactly what we can do." You glance around the mall parking lot to be sure no one can hear you. You drop your voice down to a low whisper. "You know that pet rat Larry likes to carry around in his pocket?"

"Do I? Ugh," Sid says.

"Well, we're going to steal it. When it's not with him, he keeps it in a cage in his room."

"What are we waiting for?" Joanie cries, already hurrying toward the bikes. "Let's go!"

Rush to PAGE 123.

What's a henway? You have no idea. Mr. Knowledge must be very smart.

"A hen weighs about six pounds," Mr. Knowledge says.

You groan. That old joke.

"How do you get to Carnegie Hall?" someone calls from the audience.

"Practice, practice, practice," Mr. Knowledge answers.

"Why did the chicken cross the road?" someone shouts. "Why do firemen wear red suspenders?" another person calls.

You turn to Joanie and Sid. "These are just stupid old jokes," you say. "I don't think Mr. Knowledge will be any help to us."

"Agreed," says Sid. "Let's check out Ms. Cardsharp."

You, Joanie, and Sid find a side door and sneak out of the auditorium. The door opens into a small room. The only furniture is a round table with five empty chairs placed around it. A woman with frizzy blonde hair stands in front of the table, shuffling cards.

"I'm Ms. Cardsharp," she greets you. "We've been waiting for you. Time to meet your fellow players."

Turn to PAGE 56.

The cabinet stops. *Phew!* You don't think you could have taken anymore. Your stomach settles down. Sid's face turns back to its normal color.

"That was fun!" Joanie exclaims. You glare at her.

The door to the cabinet is flung open. A woman with frizzy blonde hair smiles at you. She wears a red striped shirt, a black vest, and shiny black pants. She has a visor sitting low on her forehead. She shuffles a deck of cards.

"I hear you want to play a little cards," she says. "You've come to the right place." She talks so fast you can barely understand her. "We are just about to start a new game."

You, Joanie, and Sid step out of the cupboard. You find yourself in a small room with a large round table with five empty chairs.

The table is covered with a smooth green cloth. Yellow, red, and blue chips are piled on the edge of the table. You hear the rustling of the cards flying through Ms. Cardsharp's fingers.

"Now, meet your opponents," Ms. Cardsharp says.

Turn to PAGE 56.

40

Loud claps of thunder echo around the mall. The sky grows darker and darker. Huge cracks appear in the floor.

You watch in horror as a huge split in the tile moves toward you. Faster, faster —

"Look out!" you shout. You shove the Magic Book into the waistband of your pants. You try to outrun the widening gap but it's no use. You fall into the opening.

Your hands reach up for the edge, but the ground is shaking so much you can't get a good hold. You slide down deeper and deeper into the black hole. Your fingers scrape at the dirt along the sides. You try to find something to hold onto but there's nothing. The dirt crumbles away under your fingertips.

"Help!" you shout. But there is no one to help you.

You plunge into the earth's darkness, tumbling over, and over, and over.

Plummet to PAGE 60.

You feel someone grab your other foot. It must be Joanie. You are easily lifted upward.

Now that you think about it, you are being pulled through the hole in the ceiling awfully fast. Too fast. You have a terrible feeling that it isn't Joanie or Sid holding onto your ankle.

You're pulled through the opening in the ceiling onto the solid, hard floor. You lie there, eyes shut, too tired and too frightened to move.

But you can't put it off any longer. You have to find out if it's Sid and Joanie. You open your eyes. Nobody's there.

You untangle the rope ladder from around your feet. Then you hear a faint shuffling sound behind you.

You glance back. Three kids walk toward you. They are wearing what looks like baseball uniforms.

"Hello," you call. The kids don't answer, but keep advancing. Closer and closer.

Then you gasp. These aren't ordinary kids — they're corpses!

Turn to PAGE 90.

You watch Larry, D. J., and Buddy. You can't hear what Larry is reading from the book, but something must be funny. Everyone is laughing.

That's when you notice the rabbits.

Rabbits suddenly seem to be everywhere. They are hopping out from behind a stack of cartons on the other side of the room. One little white rabbit hops right onto the book in Larry's hands!

Larry yelps and jumps up, dropping the book. You have to cover your mouth to keep from laughing out loud. Larry the bully is afraid of a cute little bunny!

Larry's not laughing anymore. He scans the room. "Get those furry monsters!" he shouts. D. J. and Buddy jump up and begin chasing the rabbits.

They are headed right your way!

"We've got to find a place to hide," Sid hisses.

But Larry dropped the Magic Book. You spot it on the floor right where he left it — unguarded. This might be the best chance to get it back.

What should you do?

If you hide in the boxes, turn to PAGE 70.

If you make a run for the book, turn to PAGE 52.

As you near the top, you check the sand in the hourglass. Not much time left. You give Sid one last shove. He falls forward over the edge of the opening in the ceiling. You pull yourself up and over, flopping onto the floor beside him.

"No time to rest," you tell the others. "*The sand has almost run out.* We've got to find Mr. Knowledge."

As soon as you say "Mr. Knowledge," lights flash on. You are standing in the back of another theater. A drumroll announces that the performance is about to begin. You, Sid, and Joanie quickly find empty seats.

A man in a dark brown suit walks onstage. He pulls on his thin mustache and peers at the audience.

"Ask me any question," he says. "I know all the answers. I'm Mr. Knowledge."

"What's a henway?" someone shouts from the audience.

Do you know?

Yes? Go to PAGE 26.
No? Go to PAGE 38.

You are pulled through the doorway and into glaring white lights. Joanie and Sid tumble out after you.

You gaze up at the creature. You start laughing when you realize the face that scared you was only a gorilla mask!

The man takes off his mask and winks at you. He's short and bald. "Had you going there for a minute, didn't I, pardner?" he says. He sounds like your cousin from Texas.

The man drops the gorilla mask on the floor and picks up a giant cowboy hat. That's when you notice he's dressed head to toe in a cowboy outfit — jeans, cowboy boots, spurs. He helps Joanie to her feet, then shakes Sid's hand.

"You're just in time, pardner," he tells Sid.

"In time for what?" Sid asks.

"In time for some real fun," the cowboy answers.

You glance around. You are on a stage that has been decorated to look like a western ranch. Bales of hay are stacked around a fake barn door. A large wooden wheel painted red, white, and blue stands in the center of the stage.

What kind of place is this? you wonder. Then you feel something cold and hard pressed into your back.

A knife.

Go to PAGE 86.

"Why don't we play Draw?" you manage to say. You usually do well at Draw, and it's safer than trying to play a game you don't know.

Everyone seems to like the idea. Ms. Cardsharp does some fancy shuffling. Then she takes a card from the middle of the deck and places it on the table in front of her. She passes the deck to her left.

The deck of cards is passed around the table. Each person takes a card and puts it facedown on the table. Then the deck of cards reaches you. With a trembling hand, you pull a card from the deck. You take a deep breath and cross your fingers for luck.

What card did you draw?

Find a deck of playing cards. Shuffle them and then, without looking, draw one card. Put the card facedown in front of you. Then take a deep breath and turn to PAGE 74.

Get real! When has Joanie ever said anything that was of any help?

Are you having a good hair day? Because your head is going on permanent view in the Magician's collection.

THE END

"Let's go to the clubhouse," you say. "We must have something that will work." You leave your bikes at the mall. Sid can't ride with his hands locked together. Luckily, your clubhouse is only a few blocks away. You made it last summer out of the toolshed behind Sid's house.

The three of you sneak into the toolshed. Sid is handcuffed, and Joanie is hiding a stolen Magic Book in her backpack. You figure you're better off without any grown-ups around.

"Okay," you say. "Let's get to work setting Sid free. On second thought," you tease, "maybe we should keep him a prisoner a while longer."

"We can play cops and robbers," Joanie suggests. "We already know who the robber is!"

"That won't be any fun," you joke. "He's already caught!"

"Come on, guys, quit kidding around!" Sid whines. "These handcuffs are getting tighter! Really!"

You glance down at Sid's wrists. You realize he's right. The cuffs are starting to dig into his skin. They weren't doing that when he first put them on. Could they be magic handcuffs?

Turn to PAGE 83.

"Hey, what's going on over there?" It's the voice of Mr. Pool, the owner of the nearby yogurt store. D. J. lifts his foot off your hand.

"You're dead," Larry grumbles, picking himself up. "We're out of here," he tells D. J. and Buddy. "Bring the book."

D. J. yanks the book from your hand. Several pages of the book tear out. You watch them flutter to the ground.

The three bullies strut away with the Magic Book.

"Let them have the stupid book," Sid says.

"Are you all right?" Mr. Pool calls.

"Fine, thanks." You stand up and wave at him, and Mr. Pool goes back into the store.

You gather up the four pages that are scattered on the ground in front of you.

"What do you think this . . . " You stop speaking and quickly read through the first paragraph. Silently.

Oh, no! This is terrible! You gaze over at Joanie and swallow hard.

"What's wrong?" Joanie cries. "You look like you're going to be sick."

Turn to PAGE 130.

"I'll do the sawn-in-half trick," you say. At least you've seen this trick before. Who knows what a Cabinet of Swords is?

"Excellent!" The Masked Man claps his hands. The table with the long box on it rolls toward you. Taking your hand, the Masked Man helps you climb into the box.

You lie down in the hard wooden box. Your head sticks out one end. "So what do I do?" you ask. You gaze up at the Masked Man. He looks awfully nervous.

"Leave it all to me," he tells you. He ties a blindfold over your eyes and plunks the lid on the box.

"If I can just remember what I'm supposed to do," you hear the Masked Man mutter.

You don't like the sound of that!

"Hey!" you shout. You pound on the lid. "I changed my mind! I want to do the other trick!"

But no one answers. You listen hard, trying to figure out what is going on.

Then you hear the sharp teeth of a large saw slicing through the lid of the box!

Turn to PAGE 135.

"*I* can't tell you," the Masked Man continues, "but I know two people who can."

He snaps his fingers and Joanie and Sid awaken from their trance. They glance around, dazed.

"What happened?" Sid asks.

"The Masked Man is going to tell us how to get out of here," you explain.

"Good," Joanie says. "Because the sand in the hourglass has almost run out."

You hold up the tiny hourglass. It's still on the rope around your neck. You had almost forgotten about it. But Joanie is right. There is very little sand left. You are down to minutes, now.

"Who can tell us the way out?" you ask the Masked Man.

"You can ask Mr. Knowledge," he tells you. "He knows everything, and he answers all questions."

The Masked Man picks up a piece of rope and throws it into the air. The rope stiffens then rises up to the ceiling. It disappears into darkness.

"Mr. Knowledge is performing up there," he says, waving at the rope. "Or you can ask Ms. Cardsharp. She would know the way out. She's playing cards right now."

To meet Mr. Knowledge, climb the rope to **PAGE 97.**

If you want to meet Ms. Cardsharp, go to **PAGE 82.**

You are frozen in fear as you watch the Magician's hand grasping the hourglass.

Where is the rest of the Magician? you wonder.

You don't have to wait long to find out. The cape rises, rises, rises, until it towers over you. The silky fabric slips to the floor.

The Magician stands before you, one hand holding the hourglass. His other hand shoots out and grabs you by the throat.

You try to scream, but the words are choked off. The Magician's fingers squeeze tighter and tighter. The hourglass dangles in front of your eyes.

Two grains of sand left. And then it will be all over for everyone.

You must stop those grains. It's your only hope of defeating the Magician. You struggle for air and reach for the hourglass.

You miss. Your lungs are burning. You are about to pass out. You have one more chance.

You lunge for the hourglass. Do you grab it?

Close your eyes. Let your finger land on one of the numbers. Then go to that page.

77   88   77   88

"We have to grab the book now," you urge, "while Larry and his friends are chasing the rabbits!"

Larry, D. J., and Buddy race around the left side of the stack of boxes. You, Joanie, and Sid sneak around the right side. You grab the book off the floor and run.

When you reach the door, you glance back. Larry and his friends still don't notice you. They're too busy trying to catch all the rabbits.

"Hurry up," you whisper to Sid. "Open the stupid door."

"I'm trying," he says. "It's stuck, or something."

You, Sid, and Joanie all push your weight against the door.

"Going somewhere?" a voice behind you says. You stop shoving the door and turn to face Larry. Buddy and D. J. stand right behind him.

D. J. and Buddy snicker. You are trapped between the bullies and a door that won't open.

Turn to PAGE 102.

The path has turned into a slithering, slimy gigantic snake!

You slide off the back of the snake and it rears up its head and hisses at you. Its enormous tongue flicks at you. You stumble out of its reach.

This must be the Path to Doom. You've got to go back. But how? The snake slithers away. You rush back onto the stones of the path.

You run faster and faster. But you're confused, you've lost your sense of direction. Are you running back toward Safety? Or ahead to Doom?

Then you see it.

Right in front of you stands a giant scorpion. His mouth is open — waiting.

You go cold with horror. You choke down the feeling of panic in your throat. The path below you, the one you've been running on, is covered with scorpion drool.

Turn to PAGE 121.

54

When you round the back corner of the factory, you spot an old wooden door. But before you can test it, you hear music.

Rap music from a boom box.

"It's them," you whisper. "Quick! Let's hide." The three of you duck behind a pile of old tires.

Just in time! Larry, D. J., and Buddy stroll around the corner of the broken-down building. D. J. takes a long swig from a soda can. Then he crushes the can, and pitches it into an old, rusty Dumpster near the canal.

A big gray rat pokes his head over the top of the Dumpster and then leaps out. The enormous rodent is followed by another. Then another and another and another. Gross!

You hold your breath to keep from screaming. But Larry and his friends laugh. Figures. They're rats themselves!

"Let's go," Larry orders. You watch D. J. toss something gold toward the Dumpster. Then they go in the old door. Once the creeps are inside the factory, you sneak out from behind the tires.

"I think D. J. threw the Magic Book in the Dumpster," Joanie says.

"No, he didn't," Sid says. "They took the book inside with them. Let's follow them."

To search the Dumpster, turn to PAGE 120.

To sneak into the old building, turn to PAGE 12.

You hope the Cabinet of Swords won't be as deadly as it sounds.

"Let's get to work," the Masked Man commands, clapping his hands. "Now you stand there." He yanks Sid to one side of the wooden cabinet. "And you stand right there," he instructs Joanie, pulling her to the other side of the cabinet. Then he passes a hand over her face and mutters a few strange words.

Her expression goes completely blank.

He does the same thing to Sid. Sid stares into space — unmoving, unblinking.

"Wh-what did you do to them?" you stammer.

"It's for the trick!" the Masked Man informs you. "They're under my spell, of course!"

Of course.

"What kind of trick is this?" you ask.

"You'll see right now!" The Masked Man waves his hands over his head. Sid and Joanie open the doors of the tall cabinet. Inside you see the blades of ten swords running from one side of the cabinet to the other.

Somehow you don't think you're going to like being this guy's assistant.

Turn to PAGE 124.

"Meet Mr. Lucky Luck," Ms. Cardsharp announces.

A short man with bright red hair enters the room. He sits down at the table. He is wearing a shirt covered with four-leaf clovers. Rabbits' feet hang from his belt. There's a horseshoe around his neck.

"Meet Ms. Nine Lives," Ms. Cardsharp shouts.

"Meow," says a tall woman. She is dressed like a black cat. Two cat ears stick up on either side of her head.

"Meet Mr. Rambler Gambler!"

A tall man in a sparkling gold suit walks into the room and takes his seat. Diamonds sparkle on his fingers.

"Well, that's our little group," Ms. Cardsharp says. "Take a seat, and let the games begin." With that, all the other players sit down at the table.

You glance over at Sid and Joanie. They each give you a thumbs-up sign. That makes you feel a little better. You pull out a chair and sit down.

"What shall we play?" Mr. Lucky Luck asks. "How about Kaboobie? I'm lucky at Kaboobie."

Uh-oh. You've never heard of Kaboobie. What if they only play games you don't know?

Turn to PAGE 45.

You wait for Joanie's answer. "I don't have the book anymore," she finally says, her voice trembling. "I brought it back to the Magic Shop in the mall. I didn't want to disappear."

Your heart sinks into your toes. Great, you think, now I have to get to the mall and convince the Magician to help me. And I'll terrify everyone I see on the way there.

But you don't know what else you can do. You hurry to the mall.

"*AAAAAAAhhhhhh!!!!*" A woman inside a house shrieks. She yanks down the window shade. You'd better hurry. With this kind of reaction, you might be run out of town!

You stick to the alleyways, hoping to avoid terrifying too many people or animals on your way to the mall.

Finally you reach the mall. You rush to the Magic Shop.

And have the scare of your life!

Turn to PAGE 131.

Your whole body grows warm. You begin to sweat. You have the strangest feeling — as if you were glowing. And then suddenly you feel okay. Normal.

But for some reason, Joanie and Sid are staring at you in horror.

"What is it?" you cry. "Has something terrible happened? Am I green or something?"

But they don't answer you. Instead they leap out of the box and run away from you as fast as they can. They disappear behind another stack of boxes.

"Joanie? Sid?" you call after them. You wonder what scared them.

You'll have to find them later. Right now, you have a score to settle with Larry and his pals. You just hope the spell worked!

Turn to PAGE 91.

"Oops," D. J. says, dumping Joanie's stuff out of her backpack. The Magic Book falls to the ground.

"You'd better put everything back!" Joanie yells.

"Sure," Buddy replies sarcastically. Then he grabs one of her notebooks and boots it into the air like a football. D. J. spots the gold-covered Magic Book on the ground. He leans down and picks it up.

"Give that back!" you yell. You try to snatch the book out of D. J.'s hand.

"Want it?" D. J. taunts. "Catch." He throws the book to Larry. The book sails over your head.

"What's this?" Larry asks as he catches it.

Larry may be the dumbest person in school, but even Larry can tell this book is special.

"I'll just take this book with me," Larry says. "If you want it back, it will cost you $50." D. J. and Buddy start laughing.

Without thinking, you run at Larry. You slam into him. The impact knocks you both to the ground. The book flies out of Larry's hand onto the pavement. You grab for it, stretching out your fingers as far as they can reach. You've got it!

Then D. J.'s big foot comes down on your hand.

Ouch! Turn to PAGE 48.

"Wake up!" Someone is shouting into your ear. You open your eyes. Sid is standing over you.

"What happened?" you ask. "Where are we?"

"I don't know," Sid answers. "Underground somewhere?"

You rise unsteadily to your feet. You notice Joanie sitting on the floor. She looks as if she just woke up.

You glance around. The walls of the room are painted black. A wooden coffin sits on a low table. Behind it is a black velvet curtain.

"Do you think there's another brick wall behind there, like there was back at the Magic Shop?" you joke.

"Only one way to find out," Sid says.

You walk up to the curtain, unsure of what may happen next. Before you can part the thick fabric, three men dressed in red tights somersault into the room.

They reach the center of the room and begin to juggle. Balls fly through the air, faster and faster. Then, to your amazement, the balls turn into balls of fire. One of the jugglers turns your way — and throws a glowing fireball right at you!

Oh, no! Do you know how to juggle?

If you can juggle, turn to PAGE 17.
If you can't juggle, turn to PAGE 28.

You move closer to the door and listen.

"It's just the sound of the locks on the door being opened," you whisper.

"That's a lot of locks," Sid says. "Why so many?"

Before you can answer, the door opens a crack. A watery blue eye stares out at you. The door swings open wider. An orange-haired old woman steps out. She wears blue socks with high-top sneakers. She has a yellow apron over her flower-print dress.

"Hello," she says in a raspy voice. She gazes at Joanie. "What a cute little girl," she comments, patting Joanie's curls. Joanie gives the old woman one of her big smiles. The one where she shows off her dimples and flutters her eyelashes.

"What can I do for you children?" the old woman asks.

"We're friends of Larry's," you speak up. "He sent us to get Pat the Rat. He has to take Pat to the vet."

The woman's eyes squint into tiny pea holes. Her mouth pinches together tightly.

What's going on? The woman's face wrinkles up as if it is about to explode.

Go to PAGE 92.

You, Sid, and Joanie all have your eyes glued on the cup on the left. You hold your breath as Mr. Knowledge slowly, so slowly, lifts up the left cup.

The red ball rolls out.

"We win!" you cheer. You, Sid, and Joanie slap high fives. "Now, Mr. Knowledge, how do we get out of here?"

"The answer is in the red ball." He hands the small ball to you. "Throw it against the wall, and the answer will be revealed."

You hurl the ball against the wall. On impact, the ball splatters into red paint. The paint runs in all directions until it makes a doorway.

You glance down at the hourglass. Oh, no! There are just a few grains of sand left!

"Run for the door!" you shout, pushing Sid and Joanie forward. "We're almost out of time."

The three of you jump through the red doorway and find yourselves back inside the Magic Shop.

"We did it!" Sid cheers. "We're back in the mall!"

Then you hear it.

"Ha ha ha ha ha ha!"

Turn to PAGE 11.

You lost. Your card doesn't beat the king of spades.

"It's only a card game," you say, rising from the table. "We'll find our way out of here on our own."

"Not so fast," Mr. Rambler Gambler says sharply. "You have to do what I tell you. That was the rule. That's why we allowed you into the game."

You sit down. You won't go back on a promise.

Mr. Rambler Gambler leaves the room. When he comes back in, he is carrying a rhinestone suit and a paper bag.

"This is my favorite suit," Mr. Rambler Gambler tells you. "Each and every one of these little rhinestones here needs to be polished. But don't worry," he adds. "Your pals can help you." He empties the paper bag on the floor. Three baby-sized toothbrushes and a bottle of pink liquid roll out.

"I suggest you get started," Mr. Rambler Gambler says, handing you the suit.

You gaze down at the suit in your hands. There must be 4,000 rhinestones sewn onto it.

The grains of sand in the hourglass are going to run out long before you are finished cleaning the suit. You start cleaning. You almost wish the Magician would hurry up and find you. At least that way you'll come to a less boring

END.

"Before we end up on the dinner menu," Sid interrupts the jugglers, "can you take off these cuffs?"

The first juggler somersaults over to Sid. He jiggles with the cuffs. They clatter to the floor.

"How did you do that?" you ask. When you and Sid tried to unlock the handcuffs it seemed impossible.

"It's a trick," the juggler answers. "Everything is a trick here."

Suddenly all three jugglers freeze.

"The Magician," they cry together. "He's coming!"

All three disappear in a puff of smoke.

Turn to PAGE 34.

The giant reaches out for the bird in Sid's hand. The guy's hand is as big as Sid's head.

"Is my little bittle birdie okay?" The giant makes kissing sounds at the bird. "I'm a vanilla guest," he explains. "I was practicing throwing my voice."

"You mean you're a ventriloquist," Joanie corrects the man.

Good move, Joanie, you think. Get the giant mad.

The huge man peers down at Joanie.

Uh-oh, you think. Here it comes.

"You're cute," the giant tells Joanie.

"I know," she replies. They smile at each other. You don't believe it! Joanie's cute act is working on this gross guy.

"Can you show us how to get out of here?" Joanie asks, flashing her dimples.

"Come with me," the giant says, taking Joanie's hand.

"Joanie, wait," you call. You're not sure you can trust this guy.

"Do you want to just sit here and wait for the Magician?" Joanie asks you.

"She's got a point," Sid adds.

What do you think?

Should you go with the ugly giant? If so, turn to PAGE 110.

If you think it would be better to wait, go to PAGE 67.

You glance down and see that your feet are no longer touching the floor. You float higher and higher.

The Magician snaps his fingers. You are turned upside down, suspended in midair. Then you start shaking like a saltshaker.

Everything from your pants pockets falls to the ground. When the Magician is satisfied that you don't have the book, he does the same thing to Sid and Joanie. Gum wrappers, markers, rubber bands, even a sandwich fall onto the floor.

"You must have hidden the book," the Magician realizes.

THUD! You, Sid, and Joanie drop onto the floor.

"Hey!" Joanie complains. "That hurt." She rubs her backside.

"That was nothing," the Magician growls. You have a terrible feeling he is telling the truth.

The Magician claps his hands, and a tiny hourglass is suddenly hanging from a rope around your neck. "The sand will run out in exactly one hour," he explains. "If you fail to return the book in perfect condition you will join my collection."

"W-W-What collection?" you ask.

Out of nowhere, a gust of wind blows aside the velvet curtain behind the coffin. What you see makes all three of you scream in terror!

What is behind the curtain? Find out on PAGE 113.

You don't trust this guy. "No offense, but I think we should stay here," you say. You hold your breath, wondering what the giant's reaction will be.

He lets go of Joanie's hand and stalks toward you. Your eyes travel up, up, up to his gross face.

You don't believe it! There is a tear starting to trickle down his slimy cheek.

"You don't want to go with me?" the giant asks in a trembling voice. "You don't like me?" He flings himself onto the floor. His shoulders shake as he wails and moans.

"*Boo hoo hoo hoo,*" he weeps.

You, Sid, and Joanie exchange puzzled looks. "No, no, we like you a lot," you say. "Really we do."

But it's no use. The giant is crying so hard he can't even hear you. Huge tears roll onto the floor. You are soon knee-deep in tears.

Then chest-deep.

Now you can taste the giant's salty tears.

You're going under. Under.

You start crying yourself when you realize this is

THE END.

You decide to confront the Magician. You point to the remains of the book.

The Magician stares down at the torn pages. He lets out a deafening scream. His head spins completely around and sparks fly off his body.

You are frozen in terror.

He moves toward you, staggering, lurching forward. His stiff hands reach out for yours.

"Thank you, thank you, thank you," he says, shaking your hand. "By tearing up the *Magic Book of Spells*, you have released me from an evil curse."

"I did?" you say.

"Yes, you did," the Magician continues. "Now, I will do something for you. What do you want?"

"I want to go home!" you tell the Magician. "With Sid and Joanie." Then you think of something else. You whisper your request in the Magician's ear.

"No problem," the Magician assures you.

He taps you with his magic wand. A flash of green light almost blinds you. You blink a few times to clear your vision.

You're home! Sid and Joanie wave to you from your front lawn. Then Larry, D. J., and Buddy hurry down the street.

"We were so worried about you," Larry says. "You know you are our three favorite people in the whole world."

THE END

BOOM! BOOM! BOOM!

The air suddenly turns icy cold.

A noise blasts through the warehouse. It is so loud it knocks you down. You feel all squished together, like someone put you in a blender and pushed the mix button.

When you stand up, you realize that you're no longer inside the warehouse. In fact, there is no warehouse!

There's no empty lot. There's no Dumpster. There's not even any ground in front of you. There are only two narrow stone paths that arch over the nothingness.

What did I do? you wonder. You glance down at the page in the Magic Book. You read the title of the spell.

"The Spell for Two Paths — One to Safety — One to Doom."

You explain what happened to Sid and Joanie. You don't see Larry and his buddies anywhere.

"So which path do we take?" asks Sid. "Which is the Path to Safety?"

"I don't know," you answer. "The rest of the page is torn off."

Go to PAGE 107.

"The boxes!" you cry. "We can hide in the boxes."

You quickly open one of the huge boxes you've been hiding behind. All three of you scramble inside.

You hear Larry and his friends still chasing rabbits. They sound awfully close. Minutes pass.

"This is soooo boring." Joanie lets out a long sigh. "I guess I'll write in my diary."

Joanie unzips her backpack. She shifts around the books and papers until she finds her diary.

"How can you write at a time like this?" asks Sid. "You can hardly see in here it's so dark."

Sid's voice sounds a little shaky.

Joanie takes a tiny flashlight out of her pack and flicks it on. It's faint yellow beam shines dimly on Sid's face.

"Uh-oh," you whisper.

What's wrong with Sid?

Find out on PAGE 31.

"I want to use the Terrifying Spell," you say. "If I can give Larry and his buddies a good scare, maybe they won't pick on me anymore."

Joanie flips to page 71 in the Magic Book. She clears her throat. You can feel a little trickle of sweat run down your cheek as she begins to read the spell. "*Spmub. Esoog. Dooold.*" Joanie can't keep from giggling while she pronounces the strange words.

Nothing happens.

"You didn't read it right," you tell Joanie. "Stop giggling and do it again."

"I read it right," she insists. "How do you want me to read it? Like this?"

Joanie re-reads the spell. Only this time, she makes her voice sound evil and raspy.

Not bad, you think. In fact, it must have been very good because something starts to happen to you.

Turn to PAGE 58.

"Hey, Sid," you say. "Do you think Granny has a pet wolf?"

"Let's just hurry up and get out of here," Sid replies. He reaches for a sack. "These weigh a ton," he says, staggering under the weight. "Tell Joanie to give us a hand."

But Joanie is nowhere in sight.

"I'll look for her," Sid offers. He makes his way through the junk in the cellar. But after a few minutes, you don't hear him poking around anymore.

"Si-id," you call. No answer. Where is everyone? "If this is a joke," you yell, "it's not funny!"

You look at the stack of bags in front of you. The big black letters on the side of the bag stare up at you.

It can't be, you tell yourself. It *can't* be!

The bag doesn't say *Wild Wolf Chow*. It says *Werewolf Chow*.

Werewolf! A chill runs down your spine. "Sid! Joanie!" you shriek.

Then you see Granny Kapusta climbing in through the open window. Her face and arms and legs are covered with dark hair. Two fanglike teeth hang out of her mouth. She snarls at you.

You have a terrible feeling you know why Sid and Joanie disappeared. And what's about to happen to you!

THE END

You pick the cup on the left.

The three of you hold your breath, waiting to see if you're correct. So much is riding on your choice. It's your only hope of escape.

Mr. Knowledge lifts up the cup on the right. No red ball. So far so good.

"I will give you a chance to change your mind," Mr. Knowledge offers.

He places his hand on the left cup. You stare at it. Is the red ball under there?

If you want to change your mind for the middle cup, turn to PAGE 85.

If you think you should stay with the left cup, turn to PAGE 62.

Butterflies dance in your stomach as everyone at the table turns over their cards.

Ms. Cardsharp turns over the ten of clubs.

Ms. Nine Lives turns over the jack of hearts.

Mr. Rambler Gambler turns over the king of spades.

Mr. Lucky Luck turns over the five of clubs.

Your card is still facedown on the table. You are afraid to turn it over. Only an ace can beat the king. If you win, Ms. Cardsharp will have to tell you the way out. If you lose, you'll have to do whatever the winner says.

Turn over your card. Is it an ace? Did you beat the king of spades?

If you won, turn to PAGE 104.
If you lost, turn to PAGE 63.

Forget it! There is no way you are going to pay Larry $50 for a book he *stole* from you. No, you're going to find Larry and take the book back from him.

"Larry and his friends hang out at the old chemical factory," you tell Sid and Joanie. "We'll go over there, sneak in, and steal the book back."

"Great plan!" Sid cheers. You can tell he's trying to make Joanie feel better. "What are we waiting for? Let's move!"

The three of you bike to the edge of town. When you reach the old brick building, you see that most of the windows are boarded up. A battered sign is nailed to the front door. It reads DO NOT ENTER.

"How are we going to get in?" Sid whispers.

"Let's circle around back," you say.

You follow Sid and Joanie around the battered building. The brick walls are cracked and crumbling in places. An old metal fire escape covers one side of the factory. And a murky canal runs behind it.

The whole building gives you the creeps. Your parents always told you to stay away from this place. You've even heard it was *haunted*.

Turn to PAGE 54.

"Go ahead," you tell Joanie. "Use a magic spell on the dog. But it better work," you add. "This dog is about to attack!"

Joanie slips forward. The dog's eyes switch from you to her. His muscles tense. He shows Joanie his sharp, yellow teeth.

Joanie holds one of the pages torn from the Magic Book in front of her. She reads the words in a soothing tone of voice.

You watch in amazement. The dog's growls turn into little whimpers. His whole body relaxes. He lies down and rolls over. Then he sits up and holds out a paw for Joanie to shake.

Joanie starts to cross over toward the dog. You stop her. "It's a trick," you say.

"Of course, it's a trick," Sid says. Sid is climbing into the room. "She's reading a magic spell."

"I mean," you explain, "I don't believe that a few stupid words can turn a vicious dog into a pussycat."

Turn to PAGE 117.

You give it everything you've got. You stretch your arm out so far it starts to cramp. Then, using every ounce of strength you have left, you lunge for the hourglass.

You've got it! Every muscle strains as you lift the cord and place it around the Magician's neck. The hourglass dangles under his chin.

You're not too late. You watch the last piece of sand drop into the bottom of the hourglass.

The Magician's face begins to change in front of your eyes. His eyes turn up in his skull. The skin on his face bubbles like oatmeal.

You realize that the hand at your throat has relaxed its grip. It hasn't let go yet, but you can take deeper and deeper breaths. Air fills your lungs, and you begin to feel stronger.

You reach back and swing your fist at the Magician's face. The Magician's head topples off his shoulders, and bounces around on the floor! Joanie screams behind you.

But the Magician's body still has your neck in a powerful grip!

Turn to PAGE 4.

"I think we'd better give the Magician what he wants," you tell them.

Joanie and Sid nod. You sigh and walk over to the coffin.

But when you lift the lid, you discover the book has disappeared!

"It's gone!" you shout. Joanie and Sid rush over to the coffin. They peer inside.

"Maybe there's a secret compartment," Sid suggests.

You hear footsteps. They sound as if they are coming closer. And closer.

"Do you think it's the Magician?" Joanie whispers.

"I don't know, but I sure don't want to find out," you tell her. "Let's hide in the coffin."

Turn to PAGE 103.

Did you scream?

Oh, no! You *did* scream. That was the warning signal for Joanie and Sid. If they heard you, they are now walking down the other path — the real Path to Doom.

It's not too late, you tell yourself. I can save them.

"I've got to save my sister and my friend," you explain to the scorpion. "I've got to go back."

"You can't do that," the scorpion warns. "Look behind you."

You don't want to look but you must. Slowly you turn your head around. You gasp. There is no path behind you anymore.

The road has vanished. You are staring at misty empty space.

There's no way back, you think. There's no way to warn Sid and Joanie. It's all the fault of that stupid Magic Book.

You pull the book from your pocket. You rip off the covers and yank out the pages. You tear each page to shreds and throw it on the ground.

Then something weird happens. Even weirder than everything else that has happened today.

Green smoke rises up from the torn pages. You watch with fascination. Thin wisps of smoke spiral upward as each piece of paper bursts into flames.

The green smoke forms itself into a shape. What is it? What is happening?

Hurry to PAGE 133 — if you dare!

You stare at the glistening blade of the guillotine. You can't tear your eyes away. Then you notice Sid. He is taking strange stiff steps toward the terrible machine.

"Sid!" you cry. "What are you doing?" You rush over and grab his arm, but he doesn't stop.

"Ha ha ha ha ha!"

You whirl around and glare at the Magician. "Stop laughing!" you scream. "What did you do to him?" You see Joanie trembling in the corner.

"He is in my power," the Magician boasts. "There is nothing you can do."

You shake Sid, hard. He looks like a zombie. His eyes are glassy and he has the same blank expression on his face as those gruesome heads staring at you from the cabinet.

The trance must have made Sid stronger. He easily shakes you off. He lies down and places his head under the terrible blade.

"NO! Sid, no!" You glance at the hourglass dangling from the Magician's hand. Only five grains left. Time is running out.

You've got to do something. You can't stand here and watch your best friend get his head chopped off! But what?

Turn to PAGE 95, before it's too late!

Chills run down your spine. That scream sounded as if someone were being tortured.

The three of you stand perfectly still. Another loud, horrible howl screeches from somewhere above you. Then silence.

You don't like what you hear next.

Footsteps. And they are headed your way.

"Should we go back?" Joanie squeaks.

But you have no time to decide. A door opens at the other end of the steps. A face appears in the doorway.

A terrifying face. A face with slits where eyes, nose, and mouth should be. Long black stringy hair sticks out around the face and hangs down onto the creature's shoulders.

You back up into Joanie, who stumbles into Sid. "Ouch!"

"Get off!" you hear behind you. No chance of escape that way.

A large hand reaches out and grabs the front of your shirt.

"Help!" you cry.

Hurry! Turn to PAGE 44.

"We choose Ms. Cardsharp," you say enthusiastically. "I love playing cards. I'm a champion."

"At what?" Joanie says. "Go Fish?"

You ignore that remark.

"Good choice," the Masked Man tells you. "If you win, Ms. Cardsharp will tell you anything you want to know."

Something occurs to you. "What if I lose?" you ask.

"Then you must do whatever the winner wants," is his response.

I'll just have to make sure I win, you tell yourself.

The Masked Man knocks twice on the front of the sword cabinet. The door swings open. The Masked Man gestures for you to step inside. Joanie and Sid climb in behind you.

The door creaks shut. The cabinet begins to spin round and round. You're getting very dizzy. Sid is looking pretty green. If the twirling doesn't stop soon, you're going to throw up!

Turn to PAGE 39.

If those handcuffs have a spell on them, you'd better pry them off quickly. Who knows what could happen!

You gather up some tools and get to work. You insert needlenose pliers into the links of the handcuffs. You squeeze the handle as hard as you can. They don't budge.

"How about if we smash the lock?" Joanie says. She hands you a hammer. Sid eyes it nervously.

"Careful with that," he cautions you.

"Just don't move," you instruct. "Pull your hands as far apart as you can."

Sid does what you tell him. You see a bead of sweat trickle down Sid's forehead. Then he closes his eyes. You take aim and bring the hammer down as hard as you can.

SMASH!

Did it work?

Find out on PAGE 115.

You cannot move a muscle. You are frozen stiff. Granny Kapusta pries the glass of milk from your hand. You watch her but you can't do anything. You can't even blink your eyes.

The milk. There must have been something in the milk!

Granny Kapusta hurries to the cabinet and takes out a big pot. The pot matches the one already boiling on the stove. Next, she puts water, salt, and pepper in the pot. She hums as she cooks.

"I was all out of kidneys," she explains, "when the three of you showed up at my door. Now I have six fresh ones."

You listen in horror. This time when she said kidneys — you realized she was saying "kids' knees."

THE END

You are totally confused.

"It's up to you, Sid," you say. "I have no idea."

"The red ball is under the right cup," Sid insists.

You look at Mr. Knowledge's face, hoping his expression will give something away. But his face remains a blank.

"All right," you say. "We'll go with the cup on the right."

Mr. Knowledge rests his fingers lightly on the right-hand cup. He is about to lift it up when he turns to you. "Are you sure?" he asks quietly.

This is torture. Of course you're not *sure*, but you don't feel any more sure about any of the other cups. You can't wait any longer.

"The right cup!" you shout. Let's just get this over with, you think.

The cup on the right is slowly lifted.

Did you pick the correct cup?

Find out on PAGE 10.

You peer over your shoulder at the cowboy.

"Stand aside, kid," the cowboy says, flashing the knife blade at you. "You're in my light."

You don't need to be told twice. "Sorry," you mumble. You take a few steps back.

The cowboy strides toward center stage and positions himself in front of the wheel. He tosses the knife into the air and catches it behind his back. Then he tosses it up and catches it with his eyes shut. Joanie applauds.

"My, what a cute little girl," the cowboy says to Joanie. "Would you like to see another trick?"

"Sure," Joanie says. Sid nods. You don't think you ever want to see another trick in your life.

"Take your seats, take your seats," the cowboy commands, waving Sid and Joanie toward folding chairs at the side of the stage. Then he turns to you.

You have a terrible feeling that you've been chosen to be part of the cowboy's act. Right you are! The next thing you know, the cowboy is strapping you to the wooden wheel.

"You be real still," the cowboy instructs. "No wiggling."

Now what? you wonder.

Find out on PAGE 128.

Mr. Knowledge begins to move the cups around the table. He starts slowly at first, then his hands move faster and faster. He switches the middle cup with the right one. Then he moves the left cup into the middle of the other two. The cup now on the left and the cup now on the right are swapped.

You're getting dizzy watching his hands move.

"Where is the red ball?" Mr. Knowledge asks. "If you answer correctly, I will tell you what you want to know."

If you think the ball is under the cup on the right, turn to PAGE 85.

If you think the ball is still under the middle cup, turn to PAGE 15.

If you think the ball is under the cup on the left, turn to PAGE 73.

You give it all you've got, but your grasp falls just short of the hourglass.

"Joanie," you manage to gasp. "Help me. Use another spell."

As you slip in and out of consciousness, you hear Joanie reading something. But you don't understand the words.

Your eyes close. You are about to pass out when you become aware that the room is full of people. You feel the Magician yanked away from you. Your eyes flutter open.

You can't believe what you see!

The Magician is being stuffed into the cabinet by dozens of attackers — attackers who look exactly like *you*!

"Joanie!" you shout. "What did you do?"

She bites her lip. "I thought it would be a good spell." She holds out the page for you to read.

Multiply Your Strength.

It looks as if the Magician has been defeated. As soon as the cabinet door clicks into place, it disappears in a puff of smoke. The other "yous" turn and gaze at you expectantly.

It is a very weird feeling — to be stared at by dozens of faces identical to your own. What are you going to do with them?

"Great," Joanie grumbles. "As if *one* of you wasn't too many."

THE END

You are being ridiculous. Her eyes couldn't have changed color. It must have been some trick of the light. You head into the kitchen.

The weird smell is strongest in here. Granny Kapusta shuffles over to the stove and takes the cover off a big pot. She picks up a large wooden spoon and stirs the boiling mixture. Then she glances over her shoulder and winks at you.

"How about a glass of milk before you leave?" she asks. "Maybe a few cookies."

"Sure," Sid answers quickly. That figures! Sid is *always* hungry.

While Granny Kapusta gets the milk and cookies, you look around the kitchen for Pat the Rat. You hear the metal bars of a cage being rattled. The sound is coming from under the kitchen table.

Kneeling down, you reach under the table. You grab the cage and pull it toward you.

You can't believe what you see!

Turn to PAGE 126.

You stifle a scream. The corpse kids keep coming toward you. You stare at them in horror. Rotting flesh falls from their bones. Their sunken eyes stare out of their skull-like heads. They shuffle to a stop right in front of you.

"Wha-what do you want?" you stammer.

"You," one of the corpses answers.

You back up a little. Your eyes dart around, searching for a quick exit.

"Wait a minute," someone says. It's Sid.

"Sid!" you shout. "Where are you? Is Joanie all right?"

"Stop yelling," Joanie says. "We're right here."

Joanie and Sid step out from behind the three corpses.

"They asked us to play on their baseball team," Sid explains. "They need three more players."

"We joined their team," Joanie says. "They're even going to let me play first base!"

You can't believe what you are hearing. This is awful!

"Sid," you cry. "I trusted you! How could you let this happen?"

Sid hangs his head, embarrassed. He knows what you are about to say.

"I *always* play first base!"

THE END

You wonder where Larry, D. J., and Buddy are. They must have caught all the rabbits, since the furry creatures are not running around anymore.

You hear noises behind some other boxes.

"Let go of her!" Sid shouts.

"Leave me alone!" That was Joanie. Larry and his pals have cornered Joanie and Sid! Time to test this Terrifying Spell.

You rush over to the stack of boxes. Larry has his hands clenched into fists. D. J. and Buddy are sneering. Joanie and Sid cower in fear. You can't believe Larry and his friends are too stupid to notice that Joanie's ears and fingers are missing!

"Hey, you jerks!" you shout. "Leave them alone."

Larry turns at the sound of your voice. The Terrifying Spell must have worked. You watch his face go completely white. His knees actually begin knocking together.

D. J. faints, and Buddy covers his face with his hands and starts crying. Sid and Joanie also gaze at you in horror.

"Let's get out of here!" Sid exclaims. He grabs Joanie's hand, and they race out of the factory.

"You wimps!" you say to the three terrified bullies. "Don't ever bother us again."

"W-w-we wo-won't," Larry stammers.

That takes care of that, you tell yourself. You walk out of the factory smiling. But you don't smile for very long.

Turn to PAGE 96.

"*Aaa-chew!*"

The old woman sneezes. She pulls a handkerchief from her pocket and blows her nose loudly.

"My allergies," she explains. "Come in quickly or I'll be sneezing all over the three of you."

You, Sid, and Joanie follow the woman into the house.

"I'm Larry's grandmother," the woman tells you. "Granny Kapusta."

"Larry insisted we bring Pat right away," Sid says.

"That sounds like my Larry." Granny Kapusta laughs. "Always in a hurry." She pushes the three of you down a hallway. Hard!

She's a lot stronger than she looks, you think.

"Come with me," she orders. "Little Patty has been keeping me company in the kitchen. I'm making spaghetti and kidney meatballs for dinner."

Kidney meatballs? Gross. That must be what that weird smell is.

Granny Kapusta gives you another hard shove. So hard you stumble to the floor.

Trip over to PAGE 23.

You decide to climb up the rope ladder to safety. But it is a lot harder than you thought it would be!

Sid is waiting to help you. You can't see his face, but his hands reach down through the hole in the ceiling.

The climb gets harder and harder. You're moving up the rope, but only an inch at a time. Your hands begin to ache. Your arm muscles feel like mush.

"Try to swing your foot up here," you hear a whisper from above. "If we can grab hold of your foot, we can pull you up."

You have no extra breath to answer. The rope feels like it is on fire. Your shoulder muscles burn and your fingers start to cramp.

You've got to try to swing your foot up. You can't climb any longer. You're exhausted.

Slowly at first then harder and harder, you swing back and forth with the rope. You kick your legs up toward the hole.

Just when you think you are about to drop off, you feel a hand grab your ankle.

You did it! You're safe!

Turn to PAGE 41.

The dog's toothy hold has strengthened but, strangely, it doesn't hurt. This is one weird dog, you think. You take a closer look at the German shepherd. You kick your leg again. That's when the dog stops.

Just stops.

It releases your leg. You hear a whirling sound. The dog's eyes flash twice. Then he tips over, feet in the air.

You reach out a finger and lightly poke the dog. No reaction.

You pat the dog. No reaction.

You glance back at Sid and Joanie. Joanie shrugs her shoulders. Sid raises his eyebrows.

"Woof!" you bark in the dog's ear. No reaction.

Then you notice something on the dog's stomach. Something strange.

A silver wind-up mechanism.

It's a mechanical dog! It's just like a toy dog only bigger. Sid and Joanie climb through the window. Sid sets the dog back upright. The three of you roll on the floor, laughing.

Joanie kneels in front of the dog and pats its nose.

You stop laughing. Your mouth drops open in shock.

You've just noticed — Joanie's ears have disappeared!

Rush to PAGE 27.

"We'll give you the book!" you shout. "Just stop the hourglass. And release Sid!"

The Magician turns the hourglass on its side. He places it on the floor. You are relieved to see the grains of sand stop flowing through the narrow opening.

"You can't!" Joanie shrieks at you. "You can't give him back the book. He's evil. He'll use it to do evil magic."

You ignore what she says. You pull her backpack off her shoulders. The buckles open under your fingers. You grab the book.

"Bring it here," the Magician commands.

"I can't watch you do this," Joanie says. She sits by her bag and turns her back to you.

You clutch the book close to your chest with both hands. You take teeny tiny baby steps across the room.

"Quit stalling!" the Magician demands. You cross the room and stand in front of the evil man.

The Magician snatches the book from your hands. A big smirk appears on his face. But it soon turns into a grimace.

"*Bad Hare Day*," the Magician sputters, reading the title of the book out loud.

Go on to PAGE 119.

Everyone and everything flees in terror as you pass by. Dogs bark, children scream, and cats hiss.

What's going on? You glance at your reflection in a store window. You expect to see a hideous monster.

Instead you look as you always do. Nothing is different. So what makes you so terrifying?

The store owner spots you and quickly bolts his door. You have to do something fast. You must find Joanie and have her reverse the spell!

You hurry home. That's where you think Joanie will be.

But when you try to open the door, you discover it's chain-locked from the inside. "Joanie," you call through the crack in the door. "It's me! Let me in!"

"Go away!" Joanie shrieks. You peer through the tiny opening. Joanie is cowering under the dining-room table.

"It's just the spell," you explain. "As soon as you remove the spell, you won't be scared of me anymore."

"Go away!" Joanie screams again. This is going to be harder than you thought. Then you get an idea.

"Okay, Joanie, I'll go away if you'll give me the Magic Book." You can take the spell off yourself, you figure. "I'll even stand all the way by the curb. You can just slide the book through the crack in the door. Okay?" Will Joanie do it?

Turn to PAGE 57.

You decide to ask Mr. Knowledge the way out. But first you have to climb up the rope.

"You want me to climb up that rope?" Sid asks. "No way! I'm the one who gets picked last in gym for every team."

"Come on," you say. "At least you can try. Joanie and I will help you. I'll give you a boost up on my shoulders."

"It's easy," Joanie assures Sid. She scrambles up the rope and disappears into the darkness. This doesn't seem to make Sid feel any better.

You kneel down and let Sid stand on your shoulders. Slowly, slowly, you stand up. Your knees wobble.

"No more super sundaes for you, Sid," you gasp. "You weigh a ton."

"That's right," Sid says. "Tease me about my weight."

"Aw — forget it," you say. "Just climb."

Sid manages to put one hand over the other and climbs up the rope. As soon as he lifts off your shoulders, you scurry up behind him. "You can do it, Sid," you encourage him.

But can he?

Turn to PAGE 43.

Joanie opens the Magic Book to page 98. The Spell of the Genie. She reads the weird words then waits.

Ba boom!

You are shaken out of your box just in time to see the door to the warehouse crash inward. A giant enters the room. He is so tall — over eight feet — that he needs to bend his head to enter the doorway.

And he is so ugly — big boils cover his face and arms. Hair grows out of his nose and ears. The only reason that you haven't run away is because you're too scared to move. Your feet feel glued to the floor.

"Who called?" bellows the giant. "And it better be for a good reason."

Go to PAGE 109.

You gaze at the dog. Can you go back out the window before the snarling animal has you for lunch?

You tense your muscles, getting ready to sprint. The window is only four feet behind you, you tell yourself. You can reach it before the mean-looking dog in front of you takes a big chunk out of your backside.

You're about to make your move when Joanie steps up beside you.

"I can take care of this," she announces. In her hand is one of the torn-out pages from the Magic Book. "I'm going to cast a spell on the dog."

The growling dog is about to attack. You have to decide quickly!

If you want to run for the window, turn to PAGE 116.

If you think Joanie can cast a spell on the dog, turn to PAGE 76.

Joanie pulls the magic wand out of the fishbowl. You wait for something terrible to happen.

Nothing.

"It's neat the way the wand disappears when I stick it in the fishbowl," Joanie declares. She stirs the water again. "I can feel the Magic Book when I stir, but I can't see it," she adds, pulling the wet wand out of the water.

She puts the wand into the bowl a third time. She stirs so hard water splashes over the rim.

"Joanie, we have to — "

You never get a chance to finish what you were going to say. You hear a bubbling sound coming from the fishbowl. Then gurgling. Then *WHOOSH!* Water gushes out of the fishbowl. You glance at Sid. He stares at the rushing water.

Joanie shrieks and drops the wand. Water pours onto the floor, rising quickly. The painted fish come to life and start swimming in the knee-deep water.

Now you recognize what kind of fish they are.

Man-eating piranha.

Piranha aren't choosy. They don't mind being *kid*-eating piranha.

This is definitely

THE END.

You decide the coffin is the best place to hide the book. You run over to it and try to lift the lid. It won't budge.

"Help me!" you yell to Joanie and Sid. "Maybe together we can pry it open."

Joanie and Sid rush over to the coffin. Grunting and groaning, the three of you tug on the heavy lid. It gives an inch, then two inches. Enough to slip the book inside. Then the lid snaps shut, almost taking your fingers with it.

Just in time! A sound behind you makes you whirl around. You see a black hat topple off the shelf across the room. A black crow flies out. It circles the room, then lands on the coffin. You watch, stunned, as the crow turns into the Magician.

"You three meddling children have taken something of mine. I am here to get it back." The Magician's voice echoes throughout the room. He takes a step toward you. "Which one of you has my book?" he demands.

"We lost it," you say quickly.

"Don't you dare lie to me!" The whole room seems to shake with the sound of his voice. "Lies make me very angry. You don't want to see me when I'm angry," the Magician warns.

The Magician points at you. Sparks fly from his fingers. What is he doing to you?

Hurry to PAGE 66.

102

Larry takes a step toward you. You wait until he sticks his mean face right up to yours. Then you kick him in the shins. It takes him totally by surprise.

Larry yelps with pain. He hops around on one foot. He looks really silly.

Sid and Joanie start laughing. This makes you feel good.

Until you see D. J. and Buddy closing in on you.

You know the three of you are no match for the three of them. You glance down at the book in your hands. It gives you an idea.

You'll put a spell on them!

Larry stops hopping and starts coming toward you again. You hold the book in front of you and begin to read.

"*Ibin mater dos gribben datter!*" you shout.

Everyone freezes. You continue to shout the nonsense words on the page in front of you.

Nothing happens.

"*Ibin mater dos gribben dotter,*" you repeat, over and over.

"*Ibin matter!*" Larry shouts. "*Ibin matter.* You think some dumb words are going to save you?" *BOOM!!*

Turn to PAGE 69.

You, Joanie, and Sid climb into the empty coffin. The lid clicks shut above you. The three of you are squashed together.

"Watch your elbow!" Joanie snaps.

"Hey, that was my eye!" Sid complains. You get a mouthful of Joanie's hair.

You are starting to sweat. You feel as if you're going to suffocate. You have to get some air!

You place your feet on one side of the coffin and push. You try to create some space between you, Joanie, and Sid. Your shoulders press against the opposite side of the coffin. You hear a loud click.

"What was — ?" *SWOOSH!* The bottom of the coffin pops open and you are suddenly sliding down a metal chute. Faster and faster, tumbling over and over.

The chute comes to a sudden end. You crash-land onto the hard floor. Joanie and Sid hit the floor next to you.

"Look for the Magic Book!" you say, jumping up.

Joanie spots the Magic Book lying on the floor by a tall wooden cabinet. Just as she reaches for it, a man steps out from behind the cabinet. His foot lands squarely on the book.

Turn to PAGE 112.

This is it. You can't stall anymore. Everyone is waiting for you to turn over your card.

You can't look. You flip over the card with your eyes closed.

You hear loud gasps at the table.

"Hooray!" you hear Joanie shout.

"You did it!" Sid cheers.

You did it? Your eyes open wide. You look down at the card in front of you.

It's an ace! You won!

"Yes!" you cry. You jump up from your seat. Joanie and Sid throw their arms around you. The three of you jump up and down.

"I did it! I did it!" you chant.

No one at the table is moving.

"Big deal," Ms. Cardsharp says flatly. "We're playing Five Hundred Card Draw. You have to do it four hundred ninety-nine more times!"

THE END

You stare at the cover of the little gold book Joanie holds in her hand. *The Magic Book of Spells* is written in fancy writing across the cover.

"Oh, wow," you say. "Larry and his friends have been reading your diary."

"And they were laughing!" Joanie wails.

"But what about the rabbits?" Sid asks. "If Larry didn't have the Magic Book, where did all those rabbits come from?"

"Look," you say, pointing to the words on the cardboard box. *O'Connor's Pet Shop.*

"We have the Magic Book," Sid says, "so let's get out of here!"

"But how? Larry and his gang of jerks will still want to jump us," you remind him.

Joanie opens the book. "I think we should use a spell," she says. "It's the only way we'll escape."

You hate to admit it, but Joanie is probably right.

"Okay," you tell her. "But which spell?"

Joanie reads the table of contents. "I think we should use the Spell of the Genie," she suggests.

"Wait a minute," Sid says, reading over her shoulder. "How about the Terrifying Spell?"

If you want to use the Spell of the Genie, go to PAGE 98.

If you choose the Terrifying Spell, turn to PAGE 71.

106

A look of horror comes over Joanie's face as she stares at where your hand should be. Her eyes well up with tears.

"Here it is," you exclaim. You poke your hand out of your sweater. "Gotcha!" You double over, laughing.

"You have a really sick sense of humor," Joanie mutters. She sticks out her tongue and stomps away.

"Hey, now we know the book won't be seen if we put it in the fishbowl," you tell Sid. "Either the fishbowl or the water makes things invisible. We'd better put the book in something to keep it from getting wet. But what?"

Sid reaches into his pants pocket and pulls out a plastic bag. It has half of a peanut butter sandwich in it. He removes the sandwich and stuffs the whole thing into his mouth. "Here you go," he mumbles with his mouth full.

You take the Baggie from Sid and slip the book inside. Then you drop the Baggie into the fishbowl.

Joanie comes up beside you. She picks up a short black stick sitting on the shelf and taps it on the fishbowl.

"What do you think this is?" she asks.

"How should I know?" you snap. "Maybe it's the Magician's magic wand. Quit playing with it."

Joanie sticks the wand into the bowl and stirs. Oh, no! Maybe she shouldn't have done that!

Turn to PAGE 100.

Joanie grabs the book from your hand.

"There must be some clue," she says. You stare at Joanie. She is still fading! Her hands are barely visible. It almost looks as if the book is floating in the air.

"There's no time left," you say. "We've got to get the book to the Magic Shop before you disappear completely."

You have a plan. It's a simple plan. But it just might work. And it's the only way to save Joanie.

"I'll take one path," you explain. "If you hear me scream, the two of you take the other path. That will be my signal."

You stand between the two paths. "Bring the book with you," Sid says. "Maybe it can help."

You stare at the two identical stone paths. Which one should you take?

All you have to go on is luck. Is today a lucky day?

That depends on the day you are reading this book.

If today's date is even, take the left path. Turn to PAGE 111.

If today's date is odd, take the path on the right, and turn to PAGE 129.

You are positive something Joanie did was the clue to your escape. But what was it?

You retrace her steps. Sid follows right behind you. When you come to an abrupt stop, Sid bangs into you.

"I've got it!" you cry, jumping up and down.

"What?" Sid demands. "You've got what?"

"Joanie, you are fantastic!" You swoop over to her and plant a big kiss on her head. She stares up at you.

"Wh-wh-what did I do?" she stammers.

"When Joanie threw her fit, she stamped her foot," you explain. "It made a hollow sound. That means there must be a trapdoor underneath this spot on the floor."

The three of you quickly roll back the rug. There it is — a shiny metal latch in the floor. Your key to freedom!

The trapdoor opens with a creak and a groan. You can see the top of a set of stairs. A wave of damp, musty-smelling air rises up the steps.

"Come on," you say. You lead the way down the stairs.

"I can't see anything," Joanie complains behind you.

"*Shush*," you whisper. "We don't know what we'll find down here."

That's when you hear it. A bloodcurdling scream.

Go on to PAGE 81 — if you dare!

"I called you," you manage to say. "We need help escaping from here. We want to go home."

The giant genie opens his mouth and lets out a blast of laughter that sends you halfway across the room.

"You've called the wrong genie," shouts the huge genie. "I'm the Evil Genie. Humans serve *me*."

The genie reaches down and picks you up. He neatly tucks you under his arm. He is so enormous he can fit Joanie and Sid under his other arm.

"You will soon get used to your new home," he growls. "I live in a castle far from here. You will clean the castle, rake the hay, chop the firewood, and herd the cows. Of course you will also cook my meals and do anything I say."

The genie shouts a strange command. The room begins to fade away.

Well, you wanted a way out of the factory.

Now you'll have to find a way to escape from the genie!

THE END

"Okay," you tell the others. "Let's get out of here."

The giant opens a trapdoor in the floor. He pulls Joanie through it. Sid follows closely behind.

You peer into the dark hole in the floor. A damp smell makes your nose crinkle. You see crooked steps leading down.

You hope this wasn't a mistake.

You climb down the steps. You find yourself in a dark tunnel. Mold and cobwebs cling to the rough walls. The others are far ahead of you. You have to follow the sounds of their voices.

You finally come to an open doorway. You glance inside. You are met with a weird sight. Sid is sitting on the giant's knee. There's another kid sitting on the giant's other knee. The ugliest kid you've ever seen.

But you don't see Joanie anywhere. What's going on?

Rush into the room on PAGE 5.

You take one step onto the left path. You stop and glance around. So far so good. Nothing terrible has happened.

You gather up your courage and continue to walk. But slowly. Very slowly. Your hands are clenched into tight fists.

You scan ahead, looking for signs of trouble. You see someone — she stands on the path in front of you. She is wearing a silky white dress.

She is waving her hand at you. She is trying to tell you something. You can't quite hear her.

You hurry toward her.

"This is the wrong path," she says sweetly.

The wrong path! Her words echo in your ears. You try not to panic. Your body turns cold, then hot.

You've got to try to turn around. You have to run back, but your feet won't move.

A huge black tentacle wraps around your ankles. The tentacles come from beneath the woman's dress.

You hear a high-pitched laugh. The beautiful woman's face dissolves into a mass of worms.

Your heart starts pounding and you can scarcely breathe. Tentacles snap forward and wrap around your chest. They start to squeeze. And squeeze.

Turn to PAGE 13.

112

The man is tall and dressed in a sequined white suit. He wears a blue mask that covers half his face. You can tell he has no idea he is standing on the Magic Book.

You want to keep it that way.

"Welcome, welcome, welcome," the Masked Man says. "Are you my new assistants?"

"Uh, why, yes we are," you say. You glance at Joanie. She gives you a little nod. Then you wink at Sid. He winks back. He understood your plan immediately.

You approach the Masked Man and shake his hand, pulling him off the book. "Nice to meet you," you say, walking him toward Sid. You glance back to see Joanie grab the Magic Book and slip it into her backpack.

"Oh, good," the Masked Man replies. "I can never seem to keep assistants. Now come along."

The Masked Man leads you over to a low table. You don't like what you see. On it is a long, gleaming sword and a very sharp saw. A long box lies on a table nearby.

"Which trick would you like to do?" the Masked Man asks. "The Cabinet of Swords? Or would you rather be sawn in half?"

You don't like those options. But he's waiting. Choose!

To be sawn in half, turn to PAGE 49.

Try your luck in the Cabinet of Swords on PAGE 55.

You were right. Behind the curtain is a brick wall. But there's something else, too. A wooden cabinet with rows of glass shelves. And on the shelves are heads.

Human heads.

You, Sid, and Joanie stand frozen in fear. You can't tear your eyes away from the horrible sight. Twelve shrunken human heads stare back at you.

"You monster!" you shout. You force yourself to face the evil Magician.

But he disappears through the brick wall. Again.

You have to think of something. You really don't want to have your head shrunk. You don't even want to see Joanie get her annoying head shrunk.

"Now what?" Sid asks.

"Let's give back the book," Joanie says.

"I don't think we should," Sid argues. "He might not let us go after we give him what he wants. That book is our only assurance that he won't hurt us — at least for an hour," he adds, glancing at the hourglass.

"But if we don't give him the book, he'll take our heads for sure!" Joanie counters. They turn to you for a decision.

If you think you should give the book back to the Magician now, turn to PAGE 78.

If you think you'll have better luck by hanging onto the book and trying to find a way to escape, turn to PAGE 36.

"Joanie, don't move!" You race to her side. Your mom will be furious if you allowed Joanie to chop off her finger. You force yourself to look down at your sister's hand. You hope you'll be able to stand the sight of all that blood.

Joanie slowly pulls her hand from the guillotine. She grins up at you, waving all five fingers.

*Do you strangle Joanie now? Turn to PAGE 25.
Or do you use every ounce of strength and try to
ignore your little sister's tricks? Turn to PAGE 6.*

"Oh well," Joanie sighs. "I thought it was a good idea."

The handcuffs are still on Sid's wrists.

Sid stands up to search for other tools. He trips over a box. He falls to the floor — and the handcuffs snap free!

"Do you believe it?" he says, holding out his arms.

"The cuffs must open automatically if you fall," you reply. "Let's get back to the mall so we can return the handcuffs and the book."

"And get our bikes," Joanie adds.

You, Sid, and Joanie hurry back to the mall. You are just about to enter through the main doors when you hear a voice behind you. "Well, look who's here. The nerd patrol."

It's Larry Green. Larry Green is the school bully. This year he has chosen you as his latest victim.

"Go away, Larry," you say. You try to sound cool. "We don't want any trouble."

Buddy and D. J., Larry's only two friends, step out from behind some parked cars.

"We're collecting for charity," Larry tells you.

"Yeah," D. J. sneers. "Each of you gives us a donation."

"Only if you can spell donation," you joke. This makes D. J. mad. He grabs Joanie's backpack.

Oh, no! The Magic Book is in there!

Turn to PAGE 59.

Joanie has taken you completely by surprise with her goofy idea. "Are you crazy?" you snap. "Our only chance is to run for the window."

Before she can argue with you, you grab Joanie's sweater and shove her ahead of you. You race to the broken window, pushing her hard. Joanie jumps out onto the fire escape.

You're so close. You stretch your arm forward. Your fingers grab the sill. You have one foot over the edge.

Bam! The weight of the dog hits you. His powerful jaws clamp shut around your right leg. The dog yanks hard, dragging you backward into the room.

Your fingernails scratch on the dusty floor as you desperately try to resist the pull of the dog. But it's useless. There's nothing to hold onto, nothing to grab.

You twist and turn, hoping to wrench your leg free. This seems to make the dog angry. It snarls through clenched teeth, clamping down harder on your leg.

Turn to PAGE 94.

"The dog looks friendly now," you warn, "but a minute ago he was ready to take a chomp out of me."

"I think the spell worked," Sid says.

"Me, too," Joanie agrees. You notice the dog eyeing you.

"Maybe you should read that spell again," you tell Joanie. "And Sid and I will find out if the dog is really our friend."

"Good idea," Sid says.

You and Sid slowly approach the dog. You place yourselves on either side of him. "Nice doggie," you say.

Joanie reads the magic spell over again. You reach out to pat the German shepherd.

You feel the strangest sensation — as if you're shrinking inside your skin. Your body begins to shake. You fall to the floor. You roll over a few times, then sit back on your heels.

Oh, no! No! No! No! You look over at Sid. The same thing is happening to him. What spell did Joanie read?

Joanie stands over you. Her eyes are wide with shock. The paper in her hand falls to the ground.

You read the first line —

Spell to Turn One Into a Playful Dog.

THE END

118

Your eyes adjust to the semidarkness. You quickly discover the two glowing eyes belong to a mean-looking German shepherd. It bares its teeth. A low, threatening growl comes from its throat.

This is not a friendly dog.

You try to remain absolutely still. Your mom always told you that dogs can smell fear. "Uh, nice doggie?" you manage to say. The huge dog growls again.

Slowly, very slowly, you glance over your shoulder to see what Sid and Joanie are doing.

Joanie has already followed you in through the window. Now she is pressed up against the wall. Sid is still outside on the fire escape. His eyes are wide with fear.

"Back up," he calls out to you. "You can make it through the window."

You're not so sure. The window looks awfully far away.

Turn to PAGE 99.

"This is not my book!" the Magician thunders.

"Now!" you shout to Joanie. She jumps to her feet. In her hand is the *real* Magic Book. Joanie had been waiting for your signal. While you were stalling, she was searching for a magic spell that might help you.

"*No pra eet pas la nook,*" Joanie pronounces.

"Huh?" you say. You doubt the nonsense she just read will stop the Magician.

"Nooooo!" the Magician roars. His hands fly up as he tries to cover his ears. Joanie repeats the strange words.

Amazing! The spell seems to be working.

"Noooooo!" the Magician wails again. He wraps himself entirely in his cape, as if he hopes it will block out the sound of the spell. He is completely hidden inside it. Then the cape drops silently to the floor.

The Magician has vanished.

Did the spell work? That depends. Is today your lucky day? The Magic Book says Monday, Wednesday, and Friday are lucky days.

If you're reading this on a Monday, Wednesday, or Friday, turn to PAGE 134.

If you're reading this on a Tuesday, Thursday, Saturday, or Sunday, go to PAGE 24.

120

You decide to search the Dumpster. If D. J. threw away the Magic Book, then you can grab it and get out of this spooky place. When you're sure Larry and his pals are inside, you, Sid, and Joanie run to the Dumpster.

Somehow, you're elected to go into the Dumpster. You step on an old milk crate near the Dumpster and throw one leg over the metal side. You hang onto the edge, gazing at the mound of trash.

Yuck. Wads of slimy papers smeared with greasy stains clump together. Moldy food containers and banana peels rot in piles. Gross-looking things you can't even identify are scattered among boards and plaster hunks.

The smell is overpowering. The rotting garbage must have been in the Dumpster for days. You try to hold your breath as you drop onto the disgusting heap.

"Do you see the Magic Book?" Sid yells from outside the Dumpster.

"Not yet," you reply. "Wait a minute." You kick away some junk. "I think I see something with a gold cover."

You dig through the trash. There it is! You can see the Magic Book. It is lying between two rusty old metal cans.

You kneel down and reach between the two cans. The trash shifts under you. You make a desperate lunge for the book.

Turn to PAGE 29.

The giant scorpion whips his tail back and forth. You know even a regular-size scorpion has a deadly sting.

"Are you going t-t-to eat me?" you stammer. Your voice shakes with terror.

"YES, I AM," shouts the scorpion, lunging toward you.

Your legs turn to rubber. You didn't think he would really answer you! This scorpion talks!

"Just kidding," he growls. "I'm going to *save* you. Where's that cute sister of yours, and the chubby boy? I thought there were three coming."

"You mean this is the right path?" you manage to ask. It's hard to believe *this* is the Path to Safety. Giant snakes and huge talking scorpions don't make you feel very cozy.

"Yes, indeedy," the scorpion growls. "You are on the Scorpion Safetyway. Had you fooled, didn't I?"

"Ye-yes," you say. "I thought for sure I was a scorpion snack."

"Everyone does." The scorpion snickers. "That's why they all scream."

Scream? Did I scream? you wonder.

Turn to PAGE 79.

Joanie suddenly clutches your hand. Hard.

"Joanie," you whisper. "What is it? What's wrong?"

"It's — it's . . . " She can't seem to speak. She shoves her diary in your face.

"I don't want to read your dumb diary," you tell her. "It's just full of all that stupid junk you write."

She shoves the diary at you again, only harder.

"Stop it," you say firmly. "I don't have time for this. I'm trying to think of a way out of here."

You're beginning to get angry. Why does Joanie always have to act like such a jerk? Sid is about to explode. Larry and his friends have the Magic Book. It's beginning to look as if there's no way out of this mess.

Joanie's voice breaks into your thoughts.

"This isn't my diary!" she cries out. "It's the Magic Book!"

Flip to PAGE 105.

You, Sid, and Joanie have no trouble finding Larry's house. He lives in a white house with gray trim. The grass in front of the house is neatly cut and two barrels of bright red geraniums guard the steps to the front porch.

"Are you sure Larry lives here?" Sid jokes. "This looks like a place where normal people live."

Sid's right, everything looks normal. But you can't help wondering why you have such butterflies in your stomach.

You walk up the steps to the front door — then hesitate. Relax, you tell yourself. Your plan is going to work. You knock on the front door. You can hear footsteps inside.

"Just a minute," yells the person in the house. From inside comes a slow scraping sound as if someone were dragging something across a wooden floor. Again — silence.

Click! Click! Snap! Click. Swish, click.

"What's making that noise?" Joanie asks.

If you wait around to find out, turn to PAGE 61.

If you think entering Larry's house is a dangerous idea, go to PAGE 9.

You watch as Joanie and Sid silently pull each sword from the cabinet. They place them on the low table with the other gleaming sword. When all ten swords are removed, the Masked Man waves his hands again. He pronounces some more strange-sounding words. Sid and Joanie push you into the cabinet. You hear a lock snap shut.

Silence and darkness surround you. This is worse than being squished in the coffin. At least there you had Sid and Joanie for company.

And you weren't waiting to find out what those swords were going to be used for.

You don't have to wait long. Something hard and cold slides in front of your ankles. You peek down.

Yikes! It's the long blade of a sword. And there are ten more to go!

Oh, no! Go to PAGE 30.

"Great shop, Mr. Magician." You use your most polite voice. Maybe that way he won't be angry about Sid and Joanie playing with the tricks.

"Yeah! Cool stuff," Sid pipes up. He reaches out to shake the Magician's hand. What a jerk! He must have forgotten he was handcuffed!

The Magician peers down at Sid's wrists. You hear a low rumble that gradually turns into a creepy laugh.

"Sid's sorry about trying the handcuffs." You elbow Sid, so that he'll put on his most sorry face. He does.

"But we really have to get home," you continue, "so if you could get the key . . . ?"

"Key?" The Magician brings his face directly in front of yours. You notice little wisps of smoke escaping from his collar. This is getting too weird.

You glance around for Joanie. Adults usually go for her cute act. Maybe she can "cute" the Magician into getting the key.

You feel Sid tugging on your sleeve. You turn back around, but the Magician has vanished.

Where did he go?

Turn to PAGE 8.

126

Pat the Rat has doubled in size since you last saw him!

What has Larry been feeding him? you wonder.

You stare at the huge gray-and-white creature, now about the size of a loaf of bread. His long hairless tail switches back and forth.

"I see you found little Patty-cake," Granny Kapusta says, standing over you with a glass of milk.

You stand up, holding onto Pat's cage with one hand and taking the glass of milk with the other. Joanie and Sid are already sitting down at the kitchen table. Plates of cookies and half-empty glasses of milk sit in front of them.

"Come on, guys," you say, "I've got Pat. We should be going."

"Drink your milk," Granny says. "Have some cookies."

You take a sip of milk to be polite. "Come on, Joanie, get up," you say. But Joanie doesn't move. Neither does Sid. They stare blankly ahead.

That's when you notice your legs are beginning to go numb.

Turn to PAGE 84.

With a sharp jolt, you stop falling. Your foot is caught or tangled in something. You're upside down hanging by one foot. When your head stops spinning, you peer up at what saved your life.

It's a rope ladder that someone must have hung from the hole in the floor. You're suspended from the ceiling, hanging halfway into the room below.

"Are you okay?" Sid whispers above you.

"I'm fine," you mutter back. But your foot is starting to hurt. And hanging upside down is making you dizzy.

And it won't be long before Larry, D. J., and Buddy spot you.

"Quick! Climb back up," Sid says.

But the book is down there, you think. And I'm already halfway down.

You don't have much time to decide. Just take the easier route. But is it easier to go up a rope ladder or to go down one?

If you think it will be easier to go up, go to PAGE 93.

If you think it will be easier to go down, go to PAGE 20.

You watch the cowboy pick up four deadly looking knives.

Now you *know* you don't like this.

"Excuse me," you begin. But you are so frightened that you have trouble getting the words out.

The cowboy doesn't hear you. He takes three knives in his left hand. The other knife he aims directly at your head.

THWANG! The knife thuds into the wood next to your left ear. That was close.

THWANG! A second knife cuts into the wood next to your right ear. That was even closer.

"Hey! Wait a minute!" Your voice comes out as a squeak. *THWANG!* The third knife thuds right above your head.

"And now for the grand finale," the cowboy announces, "I will spin the wheel." He strides toward you.

"Let me off this thing!" you shout. But the cowboy ignores your protest. He smiles at you, grasps the side of the wheel, and gives it a sharp yank.

Round and round you turn. The cowboy takes aim with the last knife.

"Noooooo!" you wail. You can't look. You shut your eyes.

Hold your breath until you get to PAGE 35.

You gather up your courage and step onto the path. You look to the right — nothing. You look to the left — nothing.

You continue forward. You realize that you're holding your breath. It's making you dizzy.

Take a few deep breaths, you tell yourself.

You continue to walk, trying not to think about what could be ahead of you.

The road had become slick and uneven. It feels as if it is shifting under your sneakers.

You look down. The stones in the path are tiny, shiny, and slippery. In fact, the path doesn't look like a path anymore. It looks more like the skin of a —

Of a giant snake!

Race to PAGE 53.

130

You have no choice. You have to tell her.

"It's not good," you warn Joanie. Your voice trembles as you read the terrible words aloud: "The person who takes this book will have one hour to return it or disappear from this world completely."

The three of you stare at each other in silence.

"I'm going to disappear?" Joanie asks finally.

"Don't worry," you tell Joanie. "You're not going to disappear. It's just a stupid prank."

Joanie runs her hand nervously through her hair. You watch her eyes widen in terror. She lets out a piercing shriek.

"It's true," she cries. "I *am* going to disappear."

She holds her hand in front of your face. Her fingertips are gone!

"We'll get the book back, Joanie," you promise. "We just need a plan."

You figure you have two options. You could try to raise the $50 and buy the book from Larry. Or you could follow Larry and try to steal back the book.

Which should you do?

If you want to steal *back the book, turn to* PAGE 75.

If you want to buy *back the book, go to* PAGE 14.

The Magic Shop! It's gone!

You stare at the empty spot in front of you. There is no sign that the Magic Shop has ever been there.

Without the Magician and the Magic Book, you won't be able to break this Terrifying Spell. You are going to be this way forever.

Maybe you can become a star in horror movies — where everything is a scream!

THE END

"The birdcage," you decide.

"Good idea!" Sid grabs the book and races across the room. He sticks his finger into the bird-cage.

"Don't be scared, little bird," he croons. "I'm going to open your cage and put something inside."

"Hurry it up," you urge. "The Magician could be here any minute. And don't forget to put the book under the paper lining in the cage," you add. "We don't want bird 'doo-doo' all over the book."

"Stupid!"

"Of course I was going to cover the book," Sid snaps. "You don't have to call me stupid."

"I didn't!" you declare. But if you didn't, who did?

"You idiot!"

"Okay," you cry, "which one of you called me an idiot?"

"Dummies!"

"It's the bird talking!" Sid exclaims. You and Joanie rush over to the birdcage.

"Say something else, birdie," Joanie coaxes. Sid opens the cage and slips his hand inside.

That's when you hear a new voice.

"I wouldn't do that if I were you!"

Turn to PAGE 19.

You watch the green smoke as it continues to take form. Your mouth opens wider and wider in awe.

A human face appears at the top of the smoke. A face you know.

The Magician.

He's come for his book. Well, it's too late. The book is in shreds around your feet.

So this is the final showdown. What should you do?

If you let the scorpion finish him off, turn to PAGE 16.

If you confront the Magician yourself, turn to PAGE 68.

This is your lucky day.

As soon as the Magician disappears, Sid wakes up from his trance. He and Joanie race for the door.

You stand over the cape, staring at it.

It's strange to think how frightened you were, only moments before. And it was this cape that had you so scared. You pick the cape up off the floor. It is so smooth and silky, you have to wrap it around you.

It feels good. You knot the strings under your chin. You gaze down at the beautiful fabric. You begin to turn, then you twirl — faster and faster. You love the way the cape floats out behind you.

"Hey, come on," Joanie calls from the doorway.

"Let's get out of here!" Sid adds.

You turn toward their voices. Puny children. They are nothing before your great power. You know what you must do.

You snap your fingers. Behind you the cabinet door opens. You watch Sid's mouth drop open, and Joanie's eyes grow wide in terror.

"Your heads will be perfect for my collection," you tell them. The guillotine rolls farther into the room.

You have become the new Magician.

THE END

You pound harder on the box.

"Help!" you shout. "Get me out of here!"

The teeth of the saw slice back and forth, back and forth — inches from your stomach.

You can't take it anymore. You pass out.

When you open your eyes, you are still in the box. Your blindfold is off. You touch your stomach. Still in one piece. And there isn't any blood or pain. Just an odd tickling sensation.

I guess it really was just a trick, you tell yourself.

You can hear applause. "That was a great trick!" you hear Joanie say.

"Really cool," comes Sid's voice.

The lid is lifted. The Masked Man peers down at you.

"All right in there?" he asks.

"You bet!" You climb out of the box.

And immediately fall over.

What's wrong?

Find out on PAGE 21.

About the Author

R. L. STINE is the most popular author in America. Recent titles for teenagers include *I Saw You That Night!*, *Call Waiting*, *Halloween Night II*, *The Dead Girlfriend*, and *The Baby-sitter IV*, all published by Scholastic. He is also the author of the *Fear Street* series.

Bob lives in New York City with his wife, Jane, and teenage son, Matt.

GET
Goosebumps®
by R.L. Stine